Blood River

By

Barbara Pappan

Cover Design by Barbara Pappan

Copyright 2014

Edited by Dreamchasers Literary
Agency LLC

for Dreamchasers Literary Agency LLC
acting as publisher

For my family who endured my
horrendous mood swings while writing
this one: my husband, Jesse and my
daughter, Tira

Thanks for helping me make my dreams
come true

WARNING:

Blood River is an intense book with extreme levels of sex, violence and drugs. Don't read if you are under the age of eighteen or faint of heart.

As always, thanks for reading.

CHAPTER ONE

Screams echo in my ears, I gasp as I realize they are coming from my lips. My eyes feel as if they are glued shut. I can't stop clutching something, and yet I have no clue what it is I'm holding. The stench of old and new urine filter through my nostrils, and I stifle the urge to vomit.

"Shut the fuck up!" the male voice booms into my ears.

I shrink back, inside and out. My back hits a wall. I scrape my hands across the rough bricks searching for a weapon. My heart races against my spine, as small beads of sweat drip down my cheeks.

"What the hell are you doing here?" he asks.

"I don't know what you're talking about," I answer, as I find my voice.

"You came to steal from me, didn't you?"

The stench seeping from his lips is of rotten teeth, cheap tobacco and whiskey. It hits me in the face, and I stifle the urge to vomit once more. Bile hits my raw throat, burning it. Tears well up in my eyes, I blink twice to force them back but still find only blackness.

"I don't even know where I am. I can't even friggin' see." The last thing I remember doing is walking down the street looking for a taxi to take me back to Manhattan. Sighing loudly, I push myself away from the wall and toward the angry man in front of me. "Well, Dorothy, it looks like we're not in Kansas anymore."

The man grunts and pulls back. He reaches for my shoulders to balance himself and nearly topples us both.

"Who are you?" I sound braver than I feel. It's then that I realize there's a strange wetness between my legs. Searing pain wraps itself around my lower back, I grasp my abdomen and drop to my knees. *Did he rape me? Did I pee? What the hell is going on?*

7

"Just checking. Lots of people been wandering around this neighborhood, and ain't nobody knowing who's who. I figured you were here to do something stupid. Homey Joe don't likes him no stupid people in his alley."

I sigh. My hands reach for my eyes and I'm thankful to find that there's only a blindfold covering them. I pull it up sharply over my forehead. I see that I'm alone. *How? Wasn't there a man here only seconds ago? How long have I been standing here? What is so wet between my legs?*

I stare down at the crotch of my pants, and see that they're covered in blood. I want to scream but I can't. My throat aches. *How long was I screaming?*

"Don't move, Sweetie, we'll be there in two seconds," comes a soft female voice from faraway.

Staring at the blood on my hands, I swipe at the tears brimming in my eyes with the backs of my blood soaked fingers, smearing tears, dirt and blood over my eyelids and cheeks. *What the hell have I gotten myself into now?*

CHAPTER TWO

They're beside me in seconds or minutes. I don't really know. It feels as if I'm floating in time, maybe dreaming. Yeah, that's it. I'm dreaming. I have to be. Otherwise my life might really be in danger.

"Are you sure her name is Anastasia?" a male voice asks.

She pulls something from my jacket pocket and holds it up to him.

He nods and goes back to digging in the large red medical bag.

My eyes burn as the tears trickle from their corners carrying with them a layer of salt that has a mind of its own, it's all I can do to keep from reaching up and tearing at my eyes. My heart beats so loudly I'm sure the young woman beside me can hear it without the stethoscope. My breathing catches in the back of my throat, as a strong wave of pain starts in the center of my back, and pushes across my lap to the center of my belly. I gasp and grab my thighs, digging my nails into the tender flesh. I feel a scream push through my lungs, but only a grunt escapes my throat.

"Gotta get those pants off." The young man pulls heavy shears from the bag, and begins to slice the rags from my body. They lie in snatches of bloody mess between us.

Where did I get those clothes? I would never wear such nasty rags in all of my life. Who dressed me this morning?

My heart races as I stare at the top of the young man's dark head. I try to pull away, but my legs won't move. "No," I whisper.

The young woman caresses the side of my face with one hand while she grabs onto my hands with the other. She stares into my eyes, and for a second I feel at ease as I swim in her deep blue eyes. "It's all right, Anastasia. He only wants to help you. We have to see where the blood is coming from, and make sure the baby is all right."

For a glimmer of a second I recognize her face, I try to look

10

away but can't. I'm so lost. "I
... " *Who is this Anastasia she
keeps calling me? What baby? I'm
not pregnant.*

CHAPTER THREE

"Okay, the baby is coming.
When is the other unit going to
be here?" The young man removes
two aluminum foil looking
blankets from the bag.

Walkie-talkies blare in the
background but it's all white
noise to me. The whooshing of the
blood in my ears blocks out
everything.
"ETA is five minutes," she
answers.
He unfolds the first one and
places it under my legs and
bottom. The other one he opens
and lies across the tops of my
legs. "Okay, Anastasia, you are
about to have the baby. When I
tell you to push, I need you to
push. Okay?"
I glance over at him and nod
as the beginning of another pain
wave creeps up my back. I moan

softly and twist against the garbage mattress trying to get comfortable. Sweat breaks out across my forehead and trickles down my cheeks, mixing with the tears, dirt, and blood already making a path to my chin. *So this is labor. How can I be in labor? I'm not pregnant.*

"One, two, three ... push!"

With all my might, I take in a deep breath and push. The pain is so intense that for a few seconds, it feels like I have been blindfolded again. Everything is black.

"Great job, Anastasia, take a few deep breaths before the next contraction. We should have a baby in less than two minutes," the woman says with a grin.

I inhale deeply and exhale with all my might. The air burns inside my lungs and I realize it's the smell of smoke that's torturing them. It's coming from a distance, but still I smell it as if it's right beside me. One more deep breath and the pain begins again.

"All right, Anastasia, here we go. One, two, three, push!"

I bear down with all my might. It feels as if my insides

12

are ripping apart from the inside out, and I reach out to get a better grip on the woman's hand. I can't scream or yell or anything else but work to take a breath. *Breathe, breathe, breathe!*

"You're doing fantastic." The young woman squeezes my hands.

The baby cries and waves her arms wildly, as the young man wipes the mucous and blood from her face.

"You did it. You have a beautiful baby girl," he calls out. Grabbing up a rubber suction bulb, he goes to work on her nose and mouth.

Her little hands reach out, and slap at the red rubber suction bulb.

He chuckles and slips it between her feisty fingers, continuing to work on the goo. "She's definitely a fighter."

"Is … is she all right?" I ask.

"She looks great so far. We just have to keep her and you warm until the next unit gets here." The young man lays the baby in the middle of the second blanket before cutting the cord and wrapping her up. He hands her to the young woman before going back to work on my privates.

Ohmygosh, I just had a baby. I still haven't a clue who this Anastasia is they keep calling me. What the hell have I done? I stare into the face of my little daughter as the woman places her in my arms. Fresh tears streak my cheeks as my heart skips a beat. I instantly fall in love with her little face.

"You have a beautiful daughter, Anastasia. You're so lucky." The woman smiles.

"Thank you," I whisper. A part of me wants to scream "I'm not Anastasia, my name is Shoshana, Shoshana Meyers and I've never been pregnant in my life," but the only thing I can utter is another thank you.

CHAPTER FOUR

I cling to the baby in my arms as they load me on a gurney and wheel me toward the emergency vehicles. People are talking

14

around me, but they might as well be speaking Swahili because I can't seem to understand a word they're saying. All I know is there's a beautiful baby girl in my arms, and she's looking at me as seriously as I am at her.

"Hello, little girl. How are you today?"

Her brows arch and then level off. She sticks her tongue out at me. She has the darkest eyes I've ever seen and my nose.

I giggle.

The young woman reaches over and pats my arm. "We'll have you two at the hospital as quick as we can. We need to check both of you out, and make sure there are no injuries. You also need to deliver the afterbirth."

I nod. No use arguing with her or the others now. Plus, I still have no clue who she or the others are. I decide it's best to keep quiet for now. To the baby, I devote all my attention.

A young blonde woman starts working on me and the baby once we are snug inside the ambulance. Her eyes are a paler version of our rescuer but still quite beautiful. "How are we doing?

Looks like you had a big surprise today."

I stifle a chuckle. *More than you will ever know*. I nod.

"I'm going to get an IV started in case they need to give you blood once we get to the hospital. But first let me put these matching bracelets on you two so they'll know this is your baby." She grabs two identical bands and shows the numbers to me before gently wrapping one around my wrist and then the other on the baby's ankle. Seconds later, she is true to her word and pulling my left arm toward her.

I'm thankful there are rails on the gurney so I can rest my arm with the baby against it. I feel lightheaded but still unable to speak. It feels like a family of porcupines have taken up residence in my throat. All I can do is stare at the matching bracelets and coo into the baby's face. My heart gives a flutter as I realize that I'm a mommy. *I've always wanted to be a mommy, but didn't Dr. Zvago say it was impossible? A snowball's chance in hell? But then, how did I not know I was pregnant? What am I doing in East Harlem?*

16

"You did a great job out there." Blondie pats my arm and grins.

The IV is hanging from a hook above her head and she is wiping the sweat off my forehead. I want to say thank you but can't.

Two minutes later, we stop in front of the hospital and the ambulance doors are popped open. Three workers tug at the foot end of the gurney, pulling us toward them. A rush of cold air glides over me and the baby. I tug at the blanket, securing it around her to keep her warm. It takes me a second to realize we are inside and covered by several heated blankets.

My eyes close for what seems like a second, but when I open them again I can see the baby is under a warmer. The doctors and nurses are working on me. Someone has cleaned off my face because I no longer feel as if I'm wearing a mask of clay.

"Anastasia, can you hear me, Anastasia?" a male voice calls out.

I turn toward the voice and nod. "I don't think ... " I whisper. My hand reaches toward the baby.

The young woman from the alley takes it. "She's doing great, Anastasia. We just need to check her out too. You did a great job with taking care of her."

I wince as I hear my baby cry. My heart skips a beat and I glare at the nurse who is only cleaning her up. I can see she's being gentle but there are so few things I really know right now and one of them is that she's my baby. I find myself wanting to grasp onto her with all my might and just hold on for dear life.

Another nurse steps into the room and over toward me. "Hello, Anastasia?" She gasps and drops the chart. Her hands flutter to her mouth as her eyes widen. The plastic chart bounces against the bed and lands on the floor with several loud thuds. The sound echoes even in the noise filled room.

Everyone turns to stare and for an instant the room is silent.

"What the hell is wrong with you, nurse?" the burly doctor asks from across the room.

"This woman's name isn't

18

Anastasia Esterhausen," she answers and takes several steps backward, ready to bolt from the room.

"Then who is she?" the young woman from the alley asks.

"She's my sister's best friend in the whole world and she's been missing for an entire year. Her name is Shoshana, Shoshana Meyers."

CHAPTER FIVE

"Bernadette," my voice squeaks out. My hand reaches out for hers, and I'm so happy to finally see a familiar face. I try to speak again but my throat is so dry and scratchy it feels as if someone has taken wire brushes to it, scrapping it raw.

The room is still silent except for the beeping of the machines now attached to me and the baby.

Racing to my side, she grabs my hand and leans over to plant a kiss on my cheek. Tears fall from her eyes and land on my face, she reaches out and brushes them off

19

with the back of her free hand. She does the same with her own face. "Oh my gosh, we all thought you were dead. It feels like you have been gone forever. What happened to you? Where have you been for a year? A baby? How could you have a baby? I thought you weren't able to get pregnant."

"I-I-I don't know. I just know I'm here now and she's my baby," I answer, which is the truth.

Our female rescuer comes forward first, racing to Bernadette's side. She twirls my friend's sister around and is inches from her face. "Who are you and what do you mean this is Shoshana Meyers? We've been seeing her at the free women's clinic since she became pregnant. She has identification that says she's Anastasia Esterhausen."

Bernadette grins. Not once does she flinch or back down. She simply shrugs. "Who are you? My name is Bernadette Petersand. I was coming to visit one of my employees when I saw you guys unload her off the bus. At first I thought I was dreaming so I had to come see for myself. I can assure you that she is Shoshana Meyers. I can call her family, and they can identify her as well. She gave you the name Anastasia Esterhausen, right?"

Deep Blue Eyes nods and takes a step back. "My name is Emily Greene. I'm sorry for being so abrasive. She's been through so much lately, as well as being a great friend to me these last eight months. I guess I assumed you were here to hurt her. Yes, when she came in that was the name she gave."

Bernadette giggles. "I would never hurt her. I'm just happy to see her. You can't imagine all the pain her disappearance has caused within our community. I know I shouldn't have barged in, but no one was watching and I couldn't let the opportunity pass. I had to say something."

"I understand," Emily answers.

"Well, then maybe you can help us out with some of the other mysteries around this young woman, like the name," the doctor says.

"I can try. First of all, the name Anastasia Esterhausen,

it was a fake name that Karen Walker would give whenever she was trying to be anonymous. Both are characters on the show 'Will&Grace'. She used to say that she liked that name. I think she used parts of it in her books. She had thought about using it as a pen name if she ever wrote tragic love stories. I guess she found a use for it after all."

Everyone chuckles and the room fills with the noises of people doing patient care once more. Bernadette, Emily, and the doctor keep their attention on me.

"Well, then maybe you can fill in the first part of the mystery," the doctor says, as he continues to work on my privates.

"She was attacked a over year ago. I don't know all the details, as I was out of the country when it happened, but I do know she was beaten and left for dead in an alley. She had been looking at a house over on Long Island."

I squeeze her hand tightly. "No."

"No?"

"I was in New Rochelle," I

whisper.

"New Rochelle? Honey, why would you want to live there? It's so not you."

"Why do you say that?" Emily asks.

"You were house hunting, right?" Bernadette's eyebrows knit together, and she stares at me for confirmation before glancing back at Emily.

I nod a second before she looks away.

"Because she doesn't belong there." She returns her gaze toward me. "I don't know why you would want to give up your beautiful Manhattan apartment that I would die for. You've done so much with it. Really, Sweetie, it's been the envy of all of us since you moved in but you should see it now. Stan has just," she shudders, "well, I'll imagine you'll see it soon enough."

"Did she move in?" I ask, and wonder if Bernadette will even know who or what I'm talking about.

Bernadette frowns. She looks toward the baby and the others around us before gazing back at me.

"She did," I answer for her.

"Geez, girl, I'm so sorry. We all thought Stan picked up with her rather quickly after your disappearance, but no one could really say. We hunted for you for two months before the police convinced us you were dead. Only Sarah didn't believe them. She still gets on the Internet and walks the streets during the weekend. I swear she's walked the whole lower half of New York and New Jersey searching for you."

I giggle. *Sarah hates work and walking? I can't wait to see her. My best friend since we were three and were taking our first Hebrew classes together.* I sniffle as I realize a whole year is missing from my life. *A whole freaking year, where did it go?*

"So, she was attacked and taken to the hospital, then what happened?" the doctor asks.

"She was there for three days. She was unconscious but not in a coma. They had beaten her pretty badly. On that day everything was going well when one of the other patients went into cardiac arrest or something." She flutters her free hand in the air. "Anyway, when everything quieted down they went to her room to check on her and she was gone. They found video of two people dressed in black stealing her, but they had no way of finding out their faces as they were covered in black paint."

I gasp and cringe. *Why would anyone want to take me from the hospital? Who were those figures? Why would they steal a whole year of my life and leave me in an alley with a baby about to be born?*

CHAPTER SIX

Lying in the hospital bed, I never take my eyes off my baby girl. So many questions rush through my mind. I'm exhausted, physically and emotionally. It feels like I just woke up from a bad dream and a part of me wonders if I'm dreaming now. I pinch my arm and wince. *Yeah, I'm awake and alive.*

Thankfully, the police decided to post a guard at my

door for even in a hospital bed I
don't feel safe. *How could those
two have kidnapped me from the
hospital? What guts that must
take.*

"She's beautiful, isn't
she?" the nurse says, as she
ambles into the room.

I grin and nod towards her
as she makes her way toward the
baby.

"What have you decided to
call her?" She fusses with the
covers as she moves the small
basinet closer to my bedside.

"I still haven't thought of
a name. My sister is supposed to
bring me a baby name book at
three." I sit up and grab the
edge of the bassinet, pulling my
little one towards me.

The nurse takes my cue and
pushes the little bed closer to
me. "Let me help you with her."
She picks her up and lays the
baby in my arms.

My little girl coos.

"Thank you." I pull the
blanket from her face so I can

26

get a better look. *I still can't believe I gave birth to her. I'll have to give that schmuck of a doctor a call when I get home. Home. I hope I still have a home.*

"Well, I have to say I haven't seen such beautiful ladies all day," Deborah says, as she sashays into the room. One hand carries a bouquet of balloons while the other a small purse and large basket of baby goodies. Her blonde hair flutters about her face as if she is standing in front of a small fan. Not a hair out of place and makeup perfect, shimmering against her skin.

I giggle. I've never been considered the beauty in the house, Deborah was and still is. I shake my head. "You're just as goofy as ever."

The nurse helps Deborah place the goodies in one of the free chairs before taking the balloon bouquet and tying them to a small hook hanging from the ceiling.

"So that's what that is for." I snicker. "I was worried

27

that it was something you would hang me by if I didn't take care of the baby."

Everyone chuckles.

"We found that it was easier to put these hooks up for balloons so they didn't crowd around the mamas and babies. Health hazard you know. Well, unless I can get you anything I will leave you with your sister. Have a great visit." The nurse is gone before we can answer.

Waltzing over to me and the baby, Deborah plants kisses on my cheeks as well as the baby's. "She really is gorgeous and I want you to know that Moshe and I insist you come stay with us for the first six weeks after they release you. We will have a room set up downstairs with a private entrance and everything. Of course, there will be round the clock help with me at your side."

"What about Mom?" I ask, as I realize for the first time that Mom is the only name she hasn't mentioned since her visit yesterday after the baby was born. My heart skips a beat as a dark cloud begins to filter through my conscious, sitting on top of my head like a large Mexican sombrero.

Deborah slumps down in a chair and stares at the wall. A small tear trickles down her face.

"What has happened to Mom?" Tears fill my eyes, I cuddle the baby closer to my bosom as if the baby will change the words my sister might say now. My heart beat against my stomach making the Jell-O I ate an hour earlier wish to make another earthly visit through the same hole it disappeared into in the first place. I never liked being nauseated and it's even worse when you're holding a baby.

"Oh Shoshana," her hands flutter to her eyes to swipe at the tears running down her cheeks. She shakes her head. "You know after Dad died in the accident her health was going downhill. When we thought you were dead, well, she just couldn't handle it. She died six weeks after you disappeared." Her head drops to her chin as she rummages through her small handbag for a handkerchief.

It takes a minute for her words to sink in. *My mother is dead. My mother is dead and I didn't know it cause I was God knows where having God knows what happening to me. I glance down at the baby. Well, it's obvious one thing was happening besides me parading around as Anastasia Esterhausen. This is so insane. My good dream is now my nightmare.* I sigh. I want to cry but the tears of yesterday have left me drained. All I can do is blink. I realize that I'm saying "No" over and over again.

Deborah reaches for my hand, and I give it to her. She squeezes it. "I'm so sorry. I wanted to tell you yesterday but so many things were happening. I think I was still in shock at the idea that you are alive and you have a baby. I just wanted to shake you and demand you tell me where you were and why didn't you come home before now." She wipes at her flawless green eyes once more.

I swallow loudly. "I wish I had came home before now, but I'm guessing that's not easy to do when you don't know who you are or where home is."

She nods.

I clear my throat. It's still a little hoarse but not as bad as yesterday. "I-I-I hear he did it?"

"Stan did what, Sweetie?" Deborah asks, wrinkling her forehead and pursing her lips.

"Stan, he moved her in."

"That asshole. I told you he was a schmuck when you got with him. He's still a schmuck. Yes, he moved her in not long after you disappeared. The police thought he had something to do with your disappearance but since they couldn't find a body, well, they let it go." Deborah takes one more dab at her face with the white cloth before pulling a compact from her purse. She inspects her face before placing both items back in the bag.

"I may need Moshe's advice while I'm with you. After all,

Moshe is one of the best lawyers I know I know he won't stir me wrong on how to toss the freeloading garbage out of my house."

Deborah nods and stares in my direction. "Did Stan hurt you?"

I shrug. "The wonderful thing about amnesia is that you don't remember someone hurting you, but then the horrible thing about it is that you don't recall anything good either. I found out about the affair in March."

"You disappeared in April." Deborah sighs. "I know Moshe would do anything to help his favorite sister-in-law."

I snicker again. "I'm his only sister-in-law."

Deborah smiles, revealing the whitest teeth ever, nestled against dark red lips. "Now, let's get back to the most important event of the day, baby naming. I wasn't sure which rabbi you would want to officiate so we can make firm plans when you get home. I brought the book," she stands and heads toward the basket.

"What was Mom's first name?"

Deborah stops in her tracks.

"We're Ashkenazic Jews, right? Isn't it customary for Ashkenazic Jews to give their children names of the dead they wish to honor? At this moment the only thing I can think about is naming my daughter after the strongest woman I've ever known, my mom."

Deborah twirls around in her tracks and faces me again. "I know Chanah Arella was her Hebrew name and her given name was Eliyah, but everyone called her Ellie."

"Well, my little daughter," I kiss her forehead. "How do you like the name Chanah Arella, and for your Hebrew name you will be Eliyah Chanah?"

For a minute, it looks as if her lips will curl up in a grin. Her eyes shine and even in all her babyhood, I swear she understands what I'm saying.

CHAPTER SEVEN

Wrapping the snuggle tightly around Chanah, I let her soft breathing relax me. A little. Very little.

"Are you sure about this?" Deborah hands the cab driver a bill and races toward me to grab the falling bag from my hand.

"You know I am. I want to know what the hell he's been doing with my life." I let the bag slip into her waiting hands and turn around to push my way past the doorman.

The older gentleman almost passes out as his hands flutter to his mouth, he gasps. "Ms. Shoshana, I'm so happy to see you again. Ohmygosh! Is it really you?"

"You know it is, Harry," I answer. Not normally rude to the kindly gentleman, I find him quite irritating today. I almost feel sorry for him. I'm not in much of a mood to be messed with, and I know the bigger mess is still up in the penthouse with Stan's name on it. Not Harry's of course. No, it's the man who declared his love for me oh so many moons ago. How quickly he took it back afterward?

Deborah is talking a mile a minute but I hear none of it.

We ride the elevator. For a few minutes both of us are silent.

She pulls the spare the key I gave her from the small purse, and inserts it ever so slowly into the penthouse keyhole. The elevator doors slide open and we step onto the tiled floor, and face Stan and the young blonde woman I had seen him with.

She's naked except for a scrungee hanging loosely from the curls about her face. "Ohmygosh! Who the hell are you!"

He drops her slender body and bolts from the room. She scrambles to her feet, and dashes into the living room to retrieve a soft velour pink bathrobe from the couch.

I immediately recognize the bathrobe, it's mine. "Where is scared boy hiding now?"

Her lips tremble as she slips into the soft pinkness.

That was my favorite bathrobe. I'm sure going to miss

it when I have to burn it. "Where did he go?" I step over his discarded jacket. My heart is in my throat and for a second I'm blinded with rage. I stop and shake my head hoping to clear the cobwebs.

"You're her, aren't you?" Tears streak down her face, she sniffles twice before her eyes search the room for something to wipe her nose.

"There should be a clean handkerchief in the left pocket unless one of his other bimbos has used it." I sniff the air and fear invades my nostrils. Fear and the smell of urine. Instinctively, I slip a finger into the top of the baby's diaper, no wetness here. I glance over at the scared young woman just in time to see her wet herself. *Yeah, the robe is fire food now.* "I'm really not sure why you are afraid of me, or do you do this every time you get caught sleeping with someone's husband?"

She shudders and streaks toward the bathroom. Seconds later, we hear water running in the sink.

"What?" I ask, as I gaze at

my sister who's giving me 'the look'. It's a half sneer with an eye roll. It's the look that always says 'you've gone too far now'.

"You should give her the robe," she says with a grin.

I nod. "I guess I have to hunt the other guilty party. Where do you suppose he slide off to?"

Deborah points toward a trembling curtain and giggles.

I pick up the black iron poker from the fireplace and ease my way across the floor.

Baby Chanah nestles even closer to my bossom.

Raking it across the thick fabric, I bit my lip to keep from snickering.

"What the hell are you trying to do? Kill me?" Stan leaps from behind the curtain in nothing but his underwear.

Deborah cackles so loud and hard I swear she'll lay an egg any minute now.

"What have you done?" I ask. My eyes never leave his and I fight to not blink.

"What are you talking about?" he asks, stepping back into the thick fabric and wrapping it about his waist.

"No hello? No how are you?
Gee, honey I was really scared
and worried about you?" I ask.

He stumbles backward and the
metal clips tear at the fabric. A
soft ripping sound fills the air
as well as his heavy breathing.
He glares at the floor by my
feet. "Well, we all thought you
were dead. Didn't we?" He turns
to Deborah.

She throws up her hands,
shakes her head and heads for the
kitchen.

"You moved the bitch in how
long after I 'died'?" I sigh and
stroll over to the couch. I guess
having a baby takes more out of a
body than I'm used to. Slipping
into the soft comfort of the
overstuffed maroon sofa, I let
the feeling of home overtake me.
*This isn't going to be easy. I
know it's too soon but I really
have to know.* "What the fuck were
you thinking when I was out
there? That you could just
pretend I was gone, and keep
playing house in a house that
didn't even belong to you?"

Sighing loudly, Deborah
slides down into the large peach

colored recliner. She drops her
bag to the floor and stares at
Stan.

He stands like a Greek
statue, fixated to the carpet,
both hands cover his clothed
genitals as the curtains slide
freely from his grasp. He doesn't
blink, not even once, as he
stares off into space.

"Be a good host and offer us
drinks, or are you in so much
shock you have become stone?" I
giggle. The one thing you can't
really call Stan is hard, not
unless he's taking Viagra like
candy again. I glance over at
Deborah and wink.

She snickers.

"Shoshana! You really must
believe me, I love you." His body
seems to find the on switch by
itself and with a leap he is
across the room and standing
before me. Dropping to his knees,
he reaches for my free hand.

I snatch it from his fingers
and cradle the baby closer to me.
I don't want him to even breath
the air around us. My heart races
in my chest as I fight back the
desire to curse this horrible man
or get up, put the baby down, and
proceed to beat the hell out of

this wretched creature before me.
"I hate you," I whisper.

"Darling." Tears streak down
his face, he wipes at them with
the back of his hand.

"Get away from me, now." I
close my eyes, praying he will
obey. When I open them a few
minutes later he is still there
giving me his best hurt puppy dog
look. "You really need to get
your clothes on and that she-
bitch, if she is a she, out of my
freaking house before I do
something we'll both regret."

Stan rises to his feet and
takes several steps backward
almost tumbling over the glass
topped coffee table adorning the
middle of the room. "I own this
place now."

"No, you don't. You see," I
grin, "before I disappeared I
changed all my legal papers. I
knew about your little bitches
and figured what I couldn't keep
you from in a divorce settlement
I could if I were to die. You
haven't proven me dead, yet." I
chuckle. "The law still states
that a person has to be missing
seven years before declared
legally dead."

"Can I come out now?" a

small feminine voice calls from the bathroom.

"Only if you are planning to not let the door hit you on the way out," I answer.

A streak of pink and blonde hair races through the living room toward the small foyer to the elevator.

Thank God she can get out much faster than she got in.

No one says a word as the elevator bell dings twice. Swishing open, the door shuts within seconds leaving another bell ring in its wake.

"If you were smart, you would be two seconds behind her," Deborah says, rubbing her hands through the chair's velvety material.

Stan shakes his head before turning to pick up his crumbled clothes off the floor. He pushes his feet through the leggings ever so slowly, almost as if he were going to work. Another thing he wasn't always good about doing.

Fear grips my heart and I'm almost afraid to speak. Beads of sweat break out across my forehead as my mouth goes dry. "Deborah, can you see if there is any water in the kitchen?"

"Sure, Sweetie, but you call immediately if this asshole tries anything," she answers, as she jumps up and dashes toward the kitchen. She stops just long enough to wave her fist in Stan's face.

He stumbles backward again, this time slamming his calf into the glass table.

That's gotta hurt. I hope tomorrow half his leg is black and blue. "Stan, did you even try to look for me?" I know the answer even before I ask the question, but I still have to hear his lie escape his lips. I have to feel the hate and anger all over again even though at this moment I might drown from it.

"Yes," he hisses, as he lazily pulls on his shirt.

I shake my head. "Please dress quickly and leave. Let Myron Finkelstein know where you'll be staying and I'll have your things sent to you."

"Shoshana, you can't be serious." His hands rest on his hips.

"As a heart attack," I answer.

"I have my rights." Stan finishes dressing, and steps toward me once more.

"No, you don't. You need to leave before I call the police." I show him my cell phone.

"And if she doesn't call, I will," Deborah sashays back into the room carrying a tall glass of water and flashes her cell.

"I'll go, but I guarantee I'll be back. You'll regret this ... before this is all over, the penthouse, will be mine and you'll be a penniless old has-been." He's across the room and through the elevator doors with one ding.

I shake my head, "no, not in this lifetime."

CHAPTER EIGHT

Running as fast as I can, I listen to my feet slapping against the concrete. Each jolt jars them as well as my hips, sending my large boobs upward and slapping them against the air. My breath comes out in a fog, as the cold makes me shiver. I reach for my thick coat but there's none. Only a thin shirt that barely covers my arms.

My heart beats fast, pulsating the blood through my eyes and ears, begging them to explode. "Where the hell is my coat?" I shake my head and glance around at my surroundings. Trees whiz by me but I can barely see them. Tears well up in my eyes, I feel them freeze into my eyelashes. It hurts. Everything hurts.

Glancing backward, I note the shadow race across the cement and walls of the large buildings. *Who the hell is following me now?* I stagger and fall before making my way behind a large dumpster, listening intently for other footsteps. The only thing I can hear is my own breathing and heart racing in my chest, booming in my ears.

Tears streak down my face and onto my light shirt, I finally hear the sound that I've been dreading, footsteps. Loud sneaker made footsteps. *Please God, please don't let them catch me again. They'll kill me.*

Please, please make them stop. I bury my face into the collar of the shirt.

"She's over here!" one of the large men yells back. His low voice echoes against the cement and brick alleyway.

I shake my head and tremble. *Please let me be invisible.* I smell his sweet cologne even before I open my eyes and stare up into his heavy gray eyes. "Please don't do this," I whisper, as his huge hands grasp my thin shoulders and lift me up.

"You're coming with me, you crazy ass bitch. I told you there was no where you could hide that I wouldn't find you. You're going with me, Little Missy." His sausage-like fingers dig into my thin shirt, shredding it from my shoulders.

His hot breath smells like raw onions and garlic in my nostrils, and I fight back the urge to vomit. My eyes search his and all I see is hate and anger.

"Why can't you just let me go?"

Shaking his head, he grins revealing brown stained teeth. "Nah, Mr. George says I should watch you and that's just a fact, Little Missy."

I hang my head and slump down against his chest.

"You got that silly bitch?" another man hollers from somewhere.

Please let this be a dream. Please let this be a dream. A scream rips through my lungs, mouth and lips, as the second man slaps the back of my head with all his might sending stars and moons across my vision. Pain sears through my already exploding brain, I feel myself reaching for a way to hold on.

I grasp at the cloth under my hands. *Please, God, please make this stop.* Tightening my grip on the material, I let out another ear shattering scream.

A baby crying in the background pushes through my brain fog, and for a second it feels like I'm falling.

"Shoshanah, Shoshanah … wake up," a familiar female voice breaks through.

I gasp and shake my head. The crying gets louder as the pain in my brain subsides. Leaping out of bed, I stare at my surroundings. I'm not in an alley, I'm in my apartment. My apartment on Park Avenue.

My sister reaches for me.

The baby sobs softly in her bassinet.

Wrapping her arms around me as I shiver into them, I gasp and inhale deeply. I want to cry but I can't. I only need to hold my baby, and make the nightmare go away, and suddenly it dawns on me it isn't just a nightmare, but maybe a clue to what my life has been like for the last year.

CHAPTER NINE

Staring down at the front page of the New York Times, he shakes his head before slamming

47

it against the desk. *Damn hillbillies. We told them to keep a better eye on her. Now she's free and she's going to lead those asswipes straight to me. They better not if they know what is good for them.* He picks up his cell phone and hits Mr. George's special number.

"George here."

"Who's to blame for this clusterfuck?"

Mr. George clears his throat twice before answering, "I told you six months ago that she was loose, didn't I?"

"Yeah, but you also said she was still in the Appalachian Mountains, and some hillbilly had made her his wife. I was expecting her to be somewhere other than New York City."

"I … I know, sir, we really did have her under control for a while. Kept her doped up. The guys worked her over good. Ole Mickey was in love. He was on her every time he got a chance. Like watching a horny Chihuahua on your least favorite brother-in-law's leg. Hell, he was in her day and night. I think she probably didn't pee for two months."

"I told you I didn't need to know the fucking details, you low life hick. That Ole Mountain Mickey must have been the one that got her pregnant because she was found giving birth."

Silence on the other end did nothing for the man's anger.

"What about the house?"

"We took care of that. Have you seen it yet?"

Leaning against the desk, the man sighs. "I paid you and your boys for a job and now it's blowing up in my face. All I can say is it better not, or you'll be facing even bigger monsters than the ones from the mountain boys." He slams the cell back down on the desk and picks up the paper once more.

Favorite Female Horror Writer returns after living her own horror story for over a year. Amnesia has taken all of her memories away including the one of her first attack and kidnapping from the hospital. What she received in all her horror tale is a beautiful healthy baby girl and a story of which we, her readers are sure will be the basis for her next page turning thriller.

Damn, damn, damn that stupid fucking bitch. Why does she have to be a survivor? Why couldn't she be like most of the dumbass bitches … scream, run, panic, get raped and get killed?

+++++

Staring down at my computer, I shake my head and sigh. My hands poise over the keyboard, as I stare back into the bassinet at my chair side.

Chanah coos and yawns before drifting back off.

Deborah steps into the room and makes her way toward the bassinet. "What are you doing?"

"Getting reacquainted with an old friend." I trace my

fingers across the keys, as I smile at my sister.

"You really need to get your rest. I swear you tossed and turned in your sleep all night." Deborah leans over the bassinet, pulling the blanket up over the little girl's shoulder.

Sighing loudly, I grin at my sister through gritted teeth. "You know as well as I do that the only way for me to get any real sleep is for me to write. God only knows if I did any writing out there, but in here I need to keep sane. I need to write." I turn my attention back to the blank monitor staring back at me.

"You want me to watch the baby while you work?" Deborah asks.

I stare down into the bassinet before glancing first toward the door and then toward Deborah. *I barely let the nurses remove her from my sight while we were in the hospital. How can I let her leave my side even with my sister? No, I don't have to, at least not yet.* "You know, sister, I have a television in here. Plenty of books to read. Even if you get on your phone you can't disturb me while I'm writing."

Wrapping her arms around my shoulders, she hugs me tightly against her. "It's okay. I understand. How about this, if she needs to eat you take her. If she needs anything else I'll take care of her. I have a book to read. I don't get to do that at home. I'll perch my backside on the couch and make myself at home." She snuggles me in closer before kissing my cheek and making her way over to the couch. I'm guessing she doesn't want to release me anymore than I do of my sweet baby.

I return my attention to the screen and frown. The words aren't there no matter how much I will them to appear.

"By the way, your last book was a bestseller for over forty weeks."

Swinging my chair around to face Deborah, I lean toward her. "What?"

"Didn't you just sign a contract with a publisher right before the attack? I remember you telling me the editor thought it was one of your best."

My mind fogs up and begins to clear only to fog up again. A trickle of a memory eases through as I think about the last book. The last one I can recall anyway. Shaking my head, I gasp to speak but words fail me.

"Anyway, I've been reading it and I can understand why it did so well. It went off the bestseller list about a month ago. Well, since your reappearance it has once again made its way back up the charts." Picking up the large tome, Deborah flashes it toward me.

Who knew that getting kidnapped and being thought of as dead could make someone's work last that long on the bestseller list? Definitely not me, and if that's what it takes I'll take just great seller any day.

CHAPTER TEN

I stare at the words on the screen and cringe.

Racing across the sidewalk, Sammy stares at the large soup pot in her hand. She dashes around the corner, searching for the entrance. <u>How did I get outside? I was right in front of the kitchen.</u> She stumbles and flies face forward toward the sidewalk.

"Hold on, Miss," a hand reaches for her, he grasps her around the waist and brings her upright.

"I … ." She stares into his deep set blue eyes.

"You can't get in that way," a woman yells from the car.

"Come with us," he carries her to the car and they slide in.

Where did the soup go? Her eyes widen as the car

roars around three hairpin turns taking them to the back of the hotel.

"I'll take you inside." His mouth finds hers.

Sammy gasps as he helps her from the car, and they enter the building. Her screams echo as burn scarred people pass her by. "Where the hell am I?" She eyes the soup pot in her hands once more.

"You're in Hotel California, Sweetie," blue eyes answers.

"You and us," a burned woman smiles.

"You can check out any time you like but you can never leave."

"Well, I've written worse."

Deborah gazes up from her magazine. "What's that, Sweetie?"

Shaking my head, I frown at the screen once more before

gazing over at my sleeping baby. "I can't seem to get back into my writing. I don't think I've ever had a time when I couldn't just sit down and start writing.

"When is your doctor's appointment?" Deborah leans back into the overstuffed red sofa and props her feet up on the matching ottoman.

"She called earlier. She said she would stop by after doing rounds. I'm guessing that means sometime around ten tonight." Pushing my chair back, I grab a Kleenex and dab at the tears flowing down my cheeks. "Why the hell am I crying?"

Leaping to her feet and racing toward me, Deborah's arms are securely locked about my shoulders before I can say another word. "You've only been home three days. What do you expect? The baby hasn't even lost her umbilical cord clip yet and you want life to be normal. Your life hasn't been normal for a while now."

"I know," I gasp between sobs. "I just feel like I've lost

a whole year. A whole year! I can't get that back no matter how much I try."

Deborah swallows loudly. "I have to give you something." Kissing my cheek, she swipes the tears from my cheeks before stepping away from me. "I'll be right back."

"What has that silly girl done now? Huh, Chanah? Your Auntie Deborah is so silly." I glance back into the bassinet.

Chanah wrinkles up her nose, sniffing the air before sighing loudly.

"Must be nice to be a baby." I turn back toward the screen. My first instinct is to hit the delete button, but hit the save button instead. *Maybe I can make something of this trash later on.*

Bouncing into the room, Deborah pulls a large backpack from behind her back.

It's old, grubby and smells of week old trash. It bulges from all sides. It's so dirty that the original color no longer shows through.

She hands it to me. "They found this with you, Miss Anastasia Esterhausen … ," she giggles. "I mean Beaverhausen. Silly woman, you didn't even get the name right."

I crinkle my forehead and wrinkle my nose. "Huh?"

"When they found you, you had been going by the name Anastasia Esterhausen. When we used to watch "Will&Grace" together, you said that was your favorite name. I guess the bumps to your big ole noggin made you a little confused." She giggles as I take it from her.

It's heavy in my hands and I almost drop it. Staring down at the wooden floors, I cringe at the idea of putting it on the hardwood floor.

"Go ahead, put it down. It's not like you have white pile carpeting." She chuckles.

"Ohmygosh," I snicker and snort. Fighting the urge to cover my face with my hands, I shake my head and lean back as the bag slides down to the floor with a dull thud. "You aren't talking about when we were younger and one of us dumped a big glass of red Kool-Aid on Mom's white Persian rug, are you?"

Sniggering even louder than me, Deborah grasps her stomach and falls into the red cushions. She nods and grabs a throw pillow. Shoving it into her abdomen, she nods her head so hard I fear it will fly off her shoulders any second.

"It was you," I answer between gasps.

"You big liar."

Nodding, I glance toward the bassinet. Tears stream down both of my cheeks, I grab the chair sides to keep from sliding off and landing hard on the floor. "Seriously, this is making my booboos hurt." I grin.

"Seriously, you need to stop laughing and look in the bag."

"We scrubbed for hours on that damn rug to make it white again."

Pulling a handkerchief from her pocket, she dabs at her nose and eyes. "It wasn't hours, well, maybe two but the important thing was we did it. She never knew the difference."

"Yeah, that was crazy, wasn't it?" I giggle and snort once more before gasping for breath. "Okay, okay, I'll be serious now." I smirk in her direction as a flash of our baby faces with wide eyes, and hearts beating out of control. Fear dances before my eyes. "I miss Mom."

Reaching for the backpack once more, I grab it up and pull it back toward me.

Despite the filth, I make out the carpet bagger type material with a cat pattern adorning the sides. The straps are large, large enough to go over my head and rest weightlessly from under one arm. I unzip the main zipper, and prepare myself for a stench I fear it will send out when I open it.

Pulling it open, I gasp. Not only is there no stink but there is a wonderful fruity scent.

+++

"Sweetie, my sister's basement isn't too bad, is it?" Honey wraps her arms around Stan's shoulders and pulls him toward her.

"Get the fuck away from me," he hisses and pushes her off him.

Her bottom lip puffs up, and she leans against the large gray throw pillow. "Hey, you better feel lucky. This was the only place we could go until the new apartment is ready. Surely, we can make the best out of it."

Stan stares into her wide eyes and sighs. "You have no fucking idea, do you?"

Shaking her head, soft blonde curls slap against her hollow cheeks. "What do you mean?"

"We'll be lucky if we get to stay here. Your sister isn't happy and I heard her husband say we had two days to get out. Plus that bitch of wife of mine is liable to freeze all of my accounts. Her and her shyster lawyer brother-in-law will do anything to get back at me."

"Oh Stan, what about all that money you said you had stashed away just for us? Money that isn't in a bank account." She drops the pink bathrobe and pushes her large tanned breasts together letting out a soft moan. Licking her lips, she slides her foot up his leg.

"What the hell are you doing?"

"I'm trying to help you relax," she grins.

CHAPTER ELEVEN

Scratching his ass with his left hand, Ole Mickey grabs for a sandwich with his right. Tears flow down his large red cheeks. "Bubba, I don't know how I'm going to live without that woman."

Donnie Kembo cringes as he stares at the big man's feet. Shaking his head, he sighs loudly. "When are you going to get over her? She has been gone for over six months. Missy Kate has been giving your ass a lot of sass lately. I know you been fucking her, so why you stuck on that ole lady?"

Shoving the last half of the sandwich into his big mawl, Ole Mickey swipes his greasy hand through his thick black hair. "Yeah, Missy Kate could suck the chrome off a tailpipe," he winks at his cousin, "but she ain't nothing like my woman."

"That woman didn't even want to be with you. She was so fucking old. No way you could have babies with her no how." Spitting brown goo from his thin lips, Donnie Kembo swipes them with the back of his red flannel sleeve and sighs.

"What the hell do you know? Ain't like you were ever been in love. I hear tell you wuz the one who let her escape in the first place." Ole Mickey stands and glares at his smaller cousin.

Donnie Kembo's hands tremble on the porch post as he steps back. "Hey, now you know she bewitched me. How many times you see me pass out after making Moonshine? Never. I barely had a thimble full 'fore she come after me. Tole me she was gonna light up my world. Fuck, you would think as strung out as we had her on that white powder that she wouldn't be awanting to leave." He releases the post and takes two more steps backward.

Hanging his head, Ole Mickey grabs the large three by four and squeezes it tightly with both hands. "I tole you, she didn't need that shit. Why the hell did you have to give it to her in the first place?" Sweat beads pop up across his forehead and drip down his chin, Ole Mickey closes his eyes and for a second he is swaying.

"Ole Mickey?" Donnie Kembo steps forward. He swallows loudly, and reaches for the big man.

"She was mine," Ole Mickey whispers.

"I know she was, Hoss, I know she was."

"I want her back."

"I don't think that's going to happen. They got her right protected now. Chances are, she isn't even in New York City right now. She probably took one of them airplane rides to California or something. They ain't said nothing about her in a long time." Donnie Kembo's hand grazes the big man's shoulder.

Shaking his head, Ole Mickey never opens his eyes. "Nah, she's in New York City. I can feel it. Just like I kin feel your fucking neck breaking in my hands." Ole Mickey's eyes snap open as his large meat hooks wrap around the smaller man's thin neck. His thumbs jam against his cousin's windpipe and voice box silencing the man's screams even before they are uttered.

Donnie Kembo's mouth gyrates like a fishes being pulled from the water. His own hands fly toward the larger ones, as he slaps lightly against them. His

eyes bulge from their sockets as
his legs shudder beneath him.

"That's okay, Ole Mickey,
you don't have to kill him," a
deep male voice states from
behind them.

"I want my bitch back," Ole
Mickey hisses. He smirks as he
watches the man's face turn
crimson before draining itself of
all color.

"I make a deal with you,"
the man steps out onto the porch.

"What's that?" Ole Mickey
loosens his grip, allowing Donnie
Kembo to gasp for air.

The skinny man's eyes roll
into the back of his head, as he
turns blue right before inhaling
deeply. The large veins in his
neck and forehead throb out of
control.

"I know how you can get your
'bitch' back. You bring her back,
you can do anything to her and
him," he points toward the pale
man in Ole Mickey's hands.

Ole Mickey releases his
captive, and grins as his cousin

slumps to the ground unconscious. Inhaling deeply, he shakes his head and holds his nose. "That asshole always shits and pisses hisself when he gets this stupid scared. What a fucking waste of skin and bone?"

The man grins and holds out his right hand to the big man. "That's all right, better him than you. I promise you that if you do this … you'll have that wonderful life you always wanted."

+++

"I can't believe you kept this thing," I voice as my trembling hands slide across the straps. Even though I'm sitting on my knees, I feel like I'm a mile from the floor. The world sways around me and everything I look at appears to be double. Closing my eyes, I say a small prayer. "I'm so scared."

"Of course you are," Deborah drops to her knees beside me. Enveloping me in her arms, Deborah kisses my cheek.

I can hear her heart beating loudly against her fragile bones.

A small layer of perspiration slickens her hands and cheeks, Deborah gazes back toward the bassinet. Fear is the new perfume that bathes us both in its aroma, and nothing covers up that fear, not even the biggest dose of bravery.

Sighing loudly, I hug her tightly before lightly pushing her away. "Well, nothing to do but to do it."

She nods and stares at the floor beside the bag.

Opening the bag, I plunge both hands inside half expecting to scream and run from the room especially if I find anything disgusting like used condoms or syringes. I can't look. I try to prepare myself and gaze inside, but it's as if I'm blind.

My heart smashes against my breastbone, as if it is trying to dig a hole through it. Blood pulsates through my eyes and ears, I feel an intoxicating deafness and blindness I seem to get a lot lately. *Frigging blood pressure must be up, no, it's not my blood pressure that's up. It's my fear. Please, God, please let me do this. I have to do this.*

My hands grasp something hard and familiar, and I yank it free from the mass of goodies around it. Deborah and I both gasp, as we stare at the small leather bond notebook in my hands. Red. Tucked into one of the last pages is a small red ribbon.

I slide it open and tears crest in my eyes once more. I open my mouth to speak but nothing comes out. Facing my sister, I flip the book around so that she can see what I'm seeing. Not only are there words but pictures. Lots of pictures. I hadn't drawn pictures since my first novel hit the top ten. In fact I made the cover for that one. I always wanted to take time to draw but always managed to make excuses not to, but here they were … proof that my artistic side hadn't died after all. I return to the last page, the last entry and read out loud.

I need to find a new
place to camp. Already too
many people are looking at
me. I know   he is coming
for me. I can't let him find
me. I just can't. He'll hurt
the baby. He'll hurt me.

Flipping through the pages,
I'm amazed at how even when I'm
in captivity or total amnesia,
I've always managed to have some
sort of writing diary.

CHAPTER TWELVE

Picking up the baby, I
listen to her soft coos and stare
into her large brown eyes.
They're darker than the darkest
chocolate almost the same color
as her pupils. I didn't know I
could feel a love this strong in
all of my life. "Baby Girl, I
love you so much. Where have you
been all this time?"

Her lips curl up as she nuzzles against my fingertips on her cheek.

The phone rings and I glance toward the caller ID. It's my agent Bonnie.

"Who is it?" Deborah reaches for my cell, and clicks the answer button before I have a chance to tell her. "This is Shoshana's cell. How may I help you?"

She listens intently and smirks in my direction.

Turning my attention back to Chanah, I run my fingers through her thick dark hair.

"Uh huh, yeah." She picks up a notepad and pen. Jotting down a name and a few numbers, her hand moves deftly across the paper. "Now, I'm no doctor, but I really don't think she can do any interviews for another three weeks." She listens intently. "Yeah, I know they did but they weren't nearly fifty when they gave birth."

Silence.

"Well, I'll tell you what she would tell you and as I recall has told you … if she is famous now, she will be famous in three weeks. She needs complete rest and relaxation right now. After all, she has been living on the streets for way too long." She sighs and drops the pencil. Frowning, she stares up at the sky.

Silence.

I smirk at the bag in the corner. My homeless bag. Well, at least that's what I've been calling it since Deborah gave it to me.

"Seriously, Bonnie, you and I know each other, don't we?"

More silence. I know Deborah is getting an earful, but I also know Deborah will give as well as take.

"She needs time. Yeah, she has already started on a book."

I hold my breath. *Please don't tell her about the book we found a book in my bag. I don't want her to know until I've read the whole thing.* Yeah, along with the diary we found a smaller book with the basic bare bones of a new novel. I only read a few chapters but already I can tell it will be on the bestseller list as long as the last one.

"Well, she will be thrilled to know that. I can expect that there will be a check in her account within the next few days?"

I giggle. I imagine Bonnie hem-hawing around that one. She loves it when I make money, but she gives me a hard time about the money. Even when I invest she is sure I'm doing the wrong thing. I've wanted to get a new agent, but never seemed to have a chance. Grinning at my sister, I may make her my agent, after all this is said and done.

"I read the contract. I saw the numbers, girlfriend. I know exactly what her cut should be." She doodles along the edges of the page.

Leaning down, I kiss Chanah's forehead.

"I'm sure she will give him a share." Deborah rolls her eyes, and grips the desk edge with her free hand. "When did you become his agent?" An iciness escapes her lips I hadn't heard in years.

I know this can't be good.

Silence. An intense heated silence.

I sigh. I watch the veins throb in my sister's forehead and neck, and await the blowup I know is coming. Apparently Bonnie has forgotten who my sister's husband is.

Deborah nods at no one. "Okay, I'll let hubby take a look and he'll get back to you. I'll be checking the account after six tonight. If the numbers don't add up, I'll be calling you tomorrow. You have a wonderful day." With this, she clicks the off button and sets it down. Sighing loudly, she inhales deeply almost as if she's taking in the sweetest air ever.

Kissing the top of Chanah's forehead, I snuggle her more

tightly to me. "Now you know why I wanted to change agents."

Shaking her head, she pulls up the other office chair and slides down into it. "Well, she's about to find out why they call my husband 'cuda in this town. She said she couldn't send you the money because Stan's name isn't on your account. She feels that you should share the profits. That's funny considering I read the contract twice last night and nowhere does it say he gets his. What a frigging bitch."

+++

Pulling the credit card from his wallet, he slides it through the ATM slot.

"If you're looking for cash, I have your deposit right here," a deep male voice hisses from behind him.

"You know what I like." He turns around and the two men make their way to a small gray alcove.

The taller man grins and reaches into the front of his large gray overcoat. Pulling a small envelope from the top right pocket, he hands it to the other man.

Licking his lips, he takes it and stuffs it into his own right top pocket of his overcoat.

"Jackie left a small gift on the coffee table. He said you'd be much appreciative."

***

Unlocking the door, Stan grins as he pockets the key back into his wallet. *Oh yeah, I'm back.*

"Is that you, Sweetheart?" a soft female voice whispers down the hallway.

"You know it is," Stan shrugs off his overcoat, and makes his way toward the living room. Stepping inside the large room, he glances toward the coffee table and the special gift awaiting him.

A syringe lies next to a spoon and a packet of white powder.

"Nothing like Afghanistan's finest to shut the day down

right," he whispers, as he rolls up his sleeves.

"You know it, darling," she whispers, as she leans against his back. She sucks lightly on his earlobe and moans softly. "I can't wait to get you between my lips and thighs."

"If this stuff is good, I'm gonna fuck you like you ain't never been fucked before." Picking up the syringe, he checks both arms for a vein. *Oh yeah, this is gonna make it so hard. Just a little dab of Viagra with the heroin makes the dick stand up, the dick stand up … oh the dick stand up. Yes, a little dab of Viagra with heroin makes the dick stand up … in the most delightful way.* The tune plays in his head like the tune by Julie Andrews' A Little Dab of Sugar from Mary Poppins. It's all he can do to keep from smiggling and missing the vein.

Gazing hungrily at the blood pushing up into the syringe, he pushes the plunger in, and immediately feels the blood pulsating through his heart and brain. Lights explode in his eyes

77

and ears, if light could make sounds. His heart races against his breastbone, he grins as his body slumps back into the overstuffed dark sofa.

Before he can say another word he listens to the sound of his zipper sliding down. A loud zzzz echoes in the silence. Glancing down at his lap, he squints and smirks as warm, red lips envelope his manhood and pull it all the way in to the hilt. "I'm gonna skull fuck you like you were Linda Lovelace, you fucking cunt," he whispers, jamming his hands into her thick red hair. He grabs her ears and shoves her face down once more.

Her head pops up. "That's it baby, talk nasty to me. Make me cum on your dick," she squeals, as her hands drop to her mini skirt. Seconds later, she moans against his stiffness.

"That's it, bitch. Jack yourself off. I'm gonna unload my wad so far down your throat your pussy is gonna feel it."

"Oh baby, may I come now?" she gasps, squeezing her large breasts against his rod.

"You come now and I'm gonna shove my dick up your ass," he growls, grabbing her head and pulling it back toward his penis.

Tears crest in her hazel eyes as her lips quiver, she flicks out her tongue, lapping his sweat from her chin.

"Cum, bitch, cum," he grins, as he reaches down and massages her sopping wet clitoris and vaginal lips.

Grasping her large breasts, she pushes them tighter around his pole and screams. "Oh God, yes, yes, yes." Shuddering against his body, she drops her mouth back onto his penis and sucks with abandon.

"That's it. Make it hard and large, and then I'm gonna shove it up your virgin ass and really make you scream."

CHAPTER THIRTEEN

Staring down at the picture Ole Mickey gave her before she left, Candy Sue grins and licks her lips. *Yeah, this is gonna be easy peasey, lemon squeezey. I'm definitely gonna have some fun with this little darling if I can find any gal that looks something like her.*

"Five dollars," the tall woman in the doorway says, as she turns toward her. Her long blonde streaked hair is piled high atop her head. Her makeup is perfect, almost too perfect. She grins and reveals pearly whites that anyone would envy.

"You got it." Candy Sue pulls a fiver from her pocket and hands it to her, leaving her hand palm side down for the usual bar stamp.

Manicured fingers on one hand snatches the money, while the other hand deftly rolls the stamper across Candy Sue's hand. The owner never takes her eyes off Candy Sue. "You ever been here before, beautiful?"

Candy Sue shakes her head and winks. "Nah, I'm not from around here," she says in her deepest southern drawl.

"Maybe I'll see you around in a little while."

Candy Sue grins. "Maybe." *Shit, I would have to be here on a mission. Go to a bar when I got nothing better to do and no one hits on me. Never fails, when I'm on an assignment they all come out of the woodwork.* She steps into the foyer, and lets her adjust to the darkness.

"Hey, Mama, what can I do you for?" the tall blonde bartender asks.

"Zima sounds pretty good," Candy Sue answers.

"You want a cherry in that?" the tall blonde winks.

"Sure," Candy Sue nods.

The tall blonde races off, and steps back a few seconds later with a tall glass bottle, cherry juice drips into the clear liquid transforming it to a bloody red. "Here you go, Sweetie, no charge."

"Thanks." Candy Sue takes the drink and slides a fiver into the tip jar anyway. She winks at the blonde once more before making her way to a table in the corner where she has a good view of the dance floor.

It's only ten but already the dance floor is filling up with hot sweaty female bodies. All shaking and swaying to techno music.

Nothing like a drink and a bunch of Lesbos to make a Saturday night unique. Sighing softly, she takes a sip and eyes two short girls. Both are brunettes. One is a little taller than the other but not by much. Her hair is shorter. *Need her short with long hair.*

Both turn to face her. They face each other and giggle. Wrapping their arms around each other, the taller girl leans down and plants her lips on the shorter girl's.

Taking a sip, Candy Sue never takes her eyes off the show as the shorter girl reaches down and rubs the taller one's crotch.

The taller one reciprocates by cupping and squeezing the shorter one's breast.

Candy Sue grins. She half expects someone, a bouncer or even the front door person, to come along and stop the girl show, but everyone else seems to be in their own worlds. *We ain't in the Appalachians now, boys. We's in the big city. We's gonna find some hot ass and take her home to Papa.*

"Like what you see?" a deep male voice asks from behind her.

Glancing out from the corner of her eye, she keeps her main focus on the women. "Looks like a pretty good show to me,"

"You look like you like quality meat."

Snickering softly under her breath, she takes another sip from her Zima. "Hon, it's all quality meat as far as I'm concerned."

"Which is your preference?"

"I bet the short one with big boobs is pretty tasty." Candy Sue's hands drift up and down the bottle. Her heart skips a beat as her pulse throbs through her temples. "How much?"

He sniggers. "Oh, I'm not their pimp. I just like to watch good loving is all."

"Uh huh." *Where'd I hear that before? Oh yeah. Looks like I got some help on this mission.* "How are you at acquiring eight balls? I hear they's pretty popular in this neck of the woods."

"That isn't a problem and from what I understand the little one that you got your eye on is all into it."

Yeah, I thought so. This is definitely going to be easy peasey and I might actually get laid in the game as well. Eyes on the prize, ain't that what Ole Mickey tells me all the time? "Sounds good to me," Candy Sue says with a soft sigh. Taking a long pull from her drink, she checks her bottle, and notices it is almost empty.

The waitress makes a beeline toward her as well as the two women from the dance floor. The waitress places another Zima in front of her, as well as drinks for the ladies taking the other two chairs at the table.

Without a word, Candy Sue motions for the young woman to come to her.

The average sized brunette leans closer to Candy Sue, her blue eyes meeting Candy Sue's hazel ones. "Can I get you anything else?"

"I think we're good." Candy Sue slides a Benjamin Franklin into the young woman's exposed red bra top peeking out from her white blouse. Nothing like being a big spender with someone else's money.

"Oh, thank you but really, it's already taken care of," she whispers.

Putting her index finger to her lips, Candy Sue shakes her head.

The waitress frowns and cocks an eyebrow.

"You take it. You work hard. Maybe you can do something special for yourself." *Maybe you can feed your two children. You don't look like you've eaten in a month.* Candy Sue doesn't say another word as the young woman walks away. She glances back at the young women at the table and grins. *Focus, focus, focus is not just the name of a Ford car. I got to keep a watch of the bait.*

+++

Stepping out of the shower, I grab the large fluffy pink towel and begin to dry off my shoulders and back. I listen for the baby, but the monitor is silent except for the noise of the television program in the background.

I don't know what I'm so worried about. Deborah is in there with her. Chanah just ate. Why are you so worried? Why am I so worried? Because I have spent the last year of my life trying to get home, and I want us to stay here.

Finally, I swipe across the outer area of my right thigh, and gasp for the hundredth time since coming to as I stare down at the tiger tattoo. It isn't large and obnoxious, but being a conservative Jew, it isn't something I would get. Not a real tattoo.

My fingertips trace the outline. The reds, blacks and whites are so starkly dark that it's almost as if the tattoo is newer than a year old. The tiger's face stares up at me with intense golden eyes that seem to say something. I just don't know what. A hint of enlarged breasts lead me to believe she's a tigress. "Of course, why would I have a tattoo of a male tiger on my leg? Why would I have a tiger tattoo?" I grin. "Maybe instead of the Girl with the Dragon Tattoo, I'm the old lady with the tiger tattoo."

"Oh my gosh! What in the hell happened to you out there?" Deborah asks, as she steps into the bathroom.

My hands wrap the towel around my body before I have a

chance to answer. My heart skips a beat, and leaps into my throat. "I, uh." Heat rises up my neck and I find myself staring at the floor. My thoughts race through my brain, but none seem to connect to my throat. I gulp several times, as my mouth dries up like the Sahara desert. My head spins, and I glance around suddenly realizing I'm sitting on the edge of a large club toed bathtub. I inhale deeply and let my brain and heart relax.

"I'm sorry, sister, I got worried. I heard the water turn off almost an hour ago. At first I thought maybe you were primping or something. I was reading and suddenly it dawned on me that you might need help."

She slumps into the soft chair in front of the vanity table.

"I'm okay. I'm sorry. I didn't mean to jump. I didn't even see this thing until I had been home the first day. I guess I was so busy getting cleaned up and taking care of the baby." I stare back at it. "At least it isn't huge."

Deborah sighs. "I have a surgeon. As soon as you are well we can have that thing taken off."

Shaking my head, I brace myself against the porcelain. "No, I'm going to leave it on."

"But why? You know we can't have tattoos. They'll never let you be buried in Mama and Papa's cemetery. It has to be taken off," Deborah answers.

"Burn it off when I'm dead. I won't care then, but something tells me this is directly connected to where I have been this last year or so, and it's going to help me find who did this to me."

CHAPTER FOURTEEN

Leaning forward so her blouse droops open, the short girl grins. Her thick black hair flows over her shoulders. "What's your name?"
"CS, hon, and yours?"

"Maddy."

"And my name is Tommie," the other girl purrs. "You have a pretty strong southern accent. What part of Florida are you from?"

"Why I'm from Alabama, can't get any more southern than that," Candy Sue answers.

"What brings you to Miami?" Maddy plays with her straw, taking short sips.

"Well, where I'm from it's sort of frowned upon to be a lesbian. Why that could get you in all sorts of trouble. So I had a chance to come down here and see what it was really like to be a real lesbian," CS answers. She stares into the taller woman's eyes for several seconds before Tommie glances away.

"Oh God, a newbie," Tommie whispers under her breath, and stares back at the dance floor.

Candy Sue shakes her head and sighs. "Don't let this southern exterior give you the wrong impression. I've had as much sex with women as you've had, but the lifestyle, that's what I don't know about. Lots of women to do in Bug Tussle. Most of 'em is married, and not willing to accidentally get pregnant by a man. They ain't got no qualms about dropping panties for me and some of 'em could suck a quarter through a coke bottle top. I just want to have a little fun, that's all."

The waitress pops over with another round, and Candy Sue drops another bill into the woman's pocket.

"I see Virgie over by the bathroom." Tommie downs her drink, and pops out of her chair. "I'll be back." She races across the room toward a blonde wall standing in front of the bathroom door.

It takes Candy Sue a second to realize it's a woman and not a wall she's staring at. The woman is almost as tall as Ole Mickey and from the looks of her, the same bicep size and shoulder size as well. Several women besides Tommie swarm toward her, and Candy Sue bites her tongue to keep from giggling out loud. *Oh yeah, I think my competition just disappeared.* She and Maddy watch the foursome stroll into the bathroom.

Maddy sighs, drops her head,

and takes a long draw from her straw. "Well, she's outta here."

"How's that?" Candy Sue asks.

"That wall you just saw is Aaron with an A. She's a she, but she packs a wallop. It doesn't hurt that she always carries a little white candy, if you know what I mean." Maddy pushes the empty glass back and forth between her hands. Wetting them with the sweat, she lays her palms against the tops of her bare breasts.

"You all right?" Candy Sue leans closer.

"Huh?" Maddy gazes up at Candy Sue. "Oh, yeah. She was my ride home. She swore she wouldn't just leave me hanging, but every time we come here it's the same thing. Today, of all days, I really needed her. She's my best friend."

"What's going on today?"

"I'm originally from Texas. This gay couple paid me to come here and be a surrogate mother for them. Today, I signed the adoption papers so they can both be legally responsible for my little boy. Oh, I'll still get pictures and such from them. I get to visit once a month. God knows I gave them enough breast milk to last a while but I … "

" … just feel a little lonely?" Candy Sue eyes the wet spots on the front of Maddy's blouse and licks her lips. She can taste the milk on her tongue already.

Tears trickle down Maddy's cheeks, she swipes them off with the back of her hand. "He's a beautiful boy."

"If he looks anything like you then he's gorgeous." *Mustn't get too excited or I'll be scaring this baby off before I say boo and my panties are so wet right now … oh God, I'm gonna cum just staring into her eyes.* Taking another sip of her Zima, she realizes she still has a full one beside the half nursed one.

"Can we just get out of here?"

Candy Sue gulps loudly, but no one can hear it as the music jams louder. She grabs the girl's hand, and pulls her up and away from the table.

Neither says a word as they make their way to the exit. As they step out, a black stretch limo with even blacker windows pulls up in front of them. The big man in the driver's uniform steps around and opens the door. "Your car, madam." He tips his hat with one hand, and holds the door open with the other.

Candy Sue grasps Maddy's hand and helps her slide inside.

Several times, Maddy grasps the side of the seat and giggles. "I'm sorry. I'm not much of a drinker. I quit drinking, period, for three months before I got pregnant. This is the first time I've had anything more than a half a glass of wine at the baby's bris. I feel a little lightheaded." She snickers, as her body slips down against the leather seating leaving her flat on her back. Her breasts free themselves from the constraints of her bra and blouse.

"Come to Mama," Candy Sue is on her knees before either of them can say boo. Her lips find the left nipple, as her hand reaches for the right.

"Oh sweetie, don't stop," Maddy moans, as her hands caresses Candy Sue's cheeks.
+++++

Staring about the room,

Maddy lets her eyes adjust to the low lighting. *Where the hell am I? What happened last night?* She reaches up to swipe the sleep from her eyes. Her arms and legs feel so heavy, she can barely them them. Something tightens against her wrists and ankles, locking her almost in place.

"You won't be able to go too far," a familiar female voice whispers.

"Huh?" Maddy twists around on the bed, as she lifts herself up on her elbows. Chains clank against metal and drag against a wooden floor. Her eyes widen as they focus on the familiar face sitting in a rocker in the corner. "CS?"

Candy Sue nods and gazes toward the closed door.

"What the hell happened? What the hell did you go to me?"

"Sh," Candy Sue whispers, as she places an index finger across her pursed lips. Her eyes narrow as she shakes her head.

"What the hell happened?" Maddy asks more softly.

Standing up slowly, Candy Sue sighs and shuffles over to the young woman's side. Her tanned, naked body is covered in bruises.

"Oh God, it wasn't a bad dream," Maddy gasps under her breath.

"No, sweetie, it wasn't. The good news is that because of me he didn't cut off your feet and blind you. The last bitch ran away, and he has never quite gotten over that."

Maddy shudders and gulps loudly, as she stares at the chain links on her wrists and ankles. The last thing she remembered was a large man with an even larger penis pushing up inside of her with as much force as the baby pushed while he was on his way out. *Oh my God, where the hell am I? What the hell did I get myself into this time? I know I'm definitely not in Kansas or Miami anymore.*

"You're in luck. He took one look at you, and fell madly in love. Unfortunately for you, when he comes back he's going to be hornier than a bull with three peckers. If I were you I'd get some rest."

CHAPTER FIFTEEN

Staring at the words in front of me, I rub the colors on the page to see if they fade off on my fingertips. They don't. The man on the page has no face only long brown hair and a thick neck. The veins in my head throb, as I wrack my brain. *Come on, surely this picture means something, but what? Why do I have three or four of the same picture or at least the same model? This is just frigging nuts.*

"Why ain't you 'fraid of me?" a deep southern drawl voices.

Gasping, I drop the tablet on the floor and leap to my feet. I twist my body around twice, searching the room for the voice. It takes me a few seconds before I realize the voice isn't coming from someone in the room, or even someone outside the room. I stare over at the baby monitor, but it's silent.

"Why ain't you 'fraid of me, little missy?" it comes again.

I drop to my knees as my hands tremble at my side. My

heart skips a beat and it's difficult to breathe, as I listen for a reply.

"Why should I be?" the female voice answers, and I realize it's my voice. It's softer than I normally speak, but it's me nonetheless.

"I's gonna fuck you every which way but loose," he answers.

Silence.

I gasp as a picture floats into my brain like a movie on a giant screen. Me, before a blue faced giant.

"What the fuck is your problem? Why ain't you afraid?"

"You want to have sex with me?"

He grunts and places his hands on his hips. Broad hips with even bigger thighs.

Tears slip down my cheeks both in the movie and real life, I don't swipe them away in either.

"Yeah, I want to have sex with you. Why do ya think you're here?"

I shrug. "I don't know. You sure you got the right woman? I'm over forty and I look like shit. No one has wanted to have sex with me in three or four years so excuse me if I don't believe you when you say you want to have sex with me. Why should I be afraid?" I mouth the words, as the movie me voices them.

He grunts again. "Serious? Youse a beautiful woman. I'd fuck you all day long and I just might. I ain't never had a willing woman. What the fuck is that going to be like?" I shrug.

He races toward the movie me. Lifting me up like a sack of potatoes, he tosses me over his shoulder and races toward the large bed. He throws me down on the bed and starts taking my clothes off as well as his.

Then the picture is gone. The sound is on and I cringe, as I listen to the loud moans and screams of ecstasy and not fear or pain. *Well, at least now we know how the baby was made. Now all we have to do is figure out what all happened. Why was I taken? Why was I attacked?* I shake it off as the ringing phone catches my attention. I rise to my feet and race toward it before it wakes anyone in the house.

"Hey Noah, what's up?" I ask, as I click on speaker.

"I hear that you aren't ready for press yet." Noah's voice is animated. In the thirty years I've known Noah, I've never heard him this animated before.

"I need a few more weeks. I have started writing. I found an old journal in the bag they found me with and surprise, surprise … I was writing even when I couldn't remember who I was."

He chuckles. "That's no surprise to me. Have you told anyone else about the notebook?"

I sigh. "No, not really. My sister was with me when I pulled it out but otherwise … no, no one knows. Why? What's up?"

"I want you to sit on this information. I know some things about your agent, and we need to do lunch soonest. When would be a great time? Today? I can grab lunch from Zabars. I presume your sister is still staying with you," Noah says.

"That would be great. Yeah, she's here. She has been my rock. Her kids are older and don't need her as much. She feels like we need to recapture our sisterhood," I snicker. "Seriously, I had totally forgotten baby care. This is my first baby and at forty-nine. It isn't as easy as she made it look."

"Your sister is a mensch. She did have help if you recall. Your mother … I'm sorry," he whispers.

"It's okay. We went to see the grave two days ago. It hurts but I think it hurts more because I know my disappearance took her. But for now, I'm okay." Sighing, I swipe the tears coursing down my cheeks. I choke back a sob, and stare at the baby's picture on my desk. My Chanah. I love her.

"When is her naming?"

"The baby naming is Friday night," I answer.

"I presume your favorite rabbi will be officiating," he adds.

"She'll be there with bells on."

"Very nice. I'll see you in an hour." He clicks off before I have a chance to say yeah or nay. Noah, never one to mince words. Staring down at my erect nipples, I realize they aren't hard because it's time to feed the baby. I had forgotten I had once been attracted to Noah but then he married Sharona and we became "just friends".

+++

"How many times are you going to go over that file?" Kevin asks, as he watches his partner stare at the folder before her. Pictures of Shoshana Meyers stretch across her desk as well as the hospital report and DVD.

"Until I figure out who did this to her and arrest the son-of-a-bitch," Olivia answers, tossing her blonde hair out of her deep blue eyes. "We missed something."

"No shit, Sherlock. What else did you come up with?" he takes a seat in the desk across from hers. His bulging belly makes him push the chair back from the desk a little more than he likes but that's okay. Since making detective he hasn't been jogging as much as he did as a beat cop.

"I know we've stared at all of this a million times but now that she has been found it might help to take another look."

"Where's the husband looking on this one?" Kevin asks.

"Well, when this case was last worked he was staying in the couple's Manhattan penthouse. He was very remorseful and adamant about us finding the body," Olivia answers.

"Let me guess, life insurance policy?"

Olivia nods. "To the tune of ten million, BUT that isn't what has my attention. At the time she was worth way more than that alive. Since then her assets have literally doubled, almost tripled. It seems the first thing she did when she first made it big was buy her place."

"Hubby work?"

"He did. Was a model for Saks or something like that, and then was a fashion buyer for a while until he quit working about two years ago."

"Hmmm …. " Kevin leans back in his chair, cupping the back of his head in his interlocked hands.

"Everything, all investigations and police work, ends nine months ago until she showed up at the hospital a week or so ago."

"What does the captain say about you digging into this one?"

Olivia shakes her head and drops her chin. "He says that we should mark it wait and see."

"Uh huh, let me guess? Your OCD is kicking your ass and you want to be a bug in someone else's ass or ear until you solve the mystery, right Scooby Doo?"

+++

Swiping the sleep from his eyes, Stan yawns and stretches before turning over.

The blonde's body lies crumpled on the floor.

How long have I been asleep? He pushes back the sheet and sits up.

"I thought I'd have that out of the way before you got up," the redhead says, as she steps over the body. She leans down, and kisses Stan on the forehead.

He grins. "She was fun for a little while, wasn't she?"

Mary Elizabeth grins as she reaches into the closet for the burlap bag. She returns to the body, and flips the blonde over.

The girl's body is ice cold, and folded up in a fetal position. Her blue eyes are clouded over, and her mouth is wide open. Bruises cover her face and torso.

"Let me help you take care of the garbage." Stan leaps to his feet and hands the bag to her. He picks the girl's stiff body and drops it into the bag. "She sure was a screamer." Stan grins.

Mary Elizabeth takes a piece of thin nylon rope from her bathrobe pocket and ties it around the bag, dropping it back on the floor with a dull thud. "She was so fucking sweet. I think Big Man is gonna be happy with this one."

"What does he do with them?"

Mary Elizabeth eyes him with lifted eyebrows. "Do you really want to know?"

He shudders. "I don't even want to know what he means he's always ranting something about 'you just watch … someday all we's gonna have to drink from is the blood river'."

CHAPTER SIXTEEN

Tommie leans up against the bathroom wall. "Oh my God, that's some really good shit. It's totally kicking my ass and blowing my mind. I can't believe you wanted to be with me," she whispers, as she pulls herself off the king sized bed. She shudders as her hands caress the silk sheets gathered at her waist. Her small breasts peek from the top. Moaning softly and licking her lips, she rubs it against her large pink nipples. "Oh baby, you just need to come over and give me a little more sugar."

The large blonde grins, as she picks up a full syringe and heads toward Tommie. "Yeah, baby, I got what you need right here. Maybe next time you can bring your little friend with you. I bet she could make us some real good money," a soft southern drawl laces the woman's normally deep voice.

A shiver races up and down Tommie's spine. *Oh God, something is wrong. What's wrong with this picture?* She glances around the large hotel room. *Or is it a hotel room? I went into the bathroom with the girls and then I woke up here. They gave me some dope there and here. What the hell happened? Yeah, yeah, I know about the sex and dope but … oh, God, what happened? What is going to happen? Where am I?* Gasping loudly, she covers herself as tears flow down her cheeks.

"You'll be okay in a minute. You just got a little more debt to pay off, and then everything will be fine." The blonde leans down and kisses the top of Tommie's head. "You are some fine piece of ass, let me tell you. I've had some really good stuff, but man, I've never seen anyone take it like you did last night."

Gulping loudly, Tommie stares into the big woman's icy blue eyes. A Cheshire grin covers the big woman's face. "What did I do?"

Leaning in closer, Big Momma roughly tweaks Tommie's left nipple. "I got something special for you today. Unfortunately for you, you will have to be very awake for this next one, and then when it's over … so are you." Before Tommie can protest, Big Momma grasps her arm and slides the needle into a vein. Blood squirts into the hub. "Bingo."

"No, ple-e-e-eas-eas-ease …. " Tommie inhales through her mouth and nose as the familiar smell of ether invades them. The drugs course through her vein, and shoots toward her heart and lungs. Her heart skips a beat before jack hammering into her rib cage. Blood pulsates against her brain and throbs in her ear. Her nipples harden and her hands reach for them impulsively. "Fuck me." Tears fill Tommie's brain as she realizes she was just hit with meth and not cocaine.

Big Momma smirks, as she pulls a cell phone from her pocket and hits send.

Seconds later, two large men about the size of Big Momma, and the two young women from the club, join them. The two men are carrying heavy chains.

Tommie feels the tears slide down her heart, and knows she is doomed, but what did she do to deserve this?

The larger man pulls his shirt off over his head, flexing his large biceps as he does. "You see Mr. Sullivan says he's gonna make you an example. It seems you was supposed to be bringing him fresh meat, as well as taking a few product trips for him. You suddenly disappeared with about twenty thousand or more in product not to mention all the money he's out training you and setting you up. Although your little girlfriend paid part of that bill it only seems right that it should be a life for a life … her being innocent and all. You being a big fucking drugged up dyke."

Sweat drips down her forehead matting her hair, Tommie shakes her head. Big Momma rips the sheet from Tommie's body, revealing her erect nipples and swollen clitoris. *Oh, God, what the hell have they done with you, Maddy? I'm so sorry, Maddy, I'm so sorry.*

CHAPTER SEVENTEEN

A baby crying pulls her from a deep sleep, Maddy stares down at her full, rock hard breasts. They're swollen to three times their normal size even when engorged, and today they ache. Milk dribbles from each nipple, and Maddy touches them gingerly as a deep seated pain sears through them almost reaching her brain. *Usually by now Candy Sue or Ole Mickey has milked them. They say it makes them all warm and powerful inside, fucking nutcakes. Usually they are right on top of me day and night. Now when I frigging need them, where are they?*

Closing her eyes, she stands and stumbles over a stool. She opens her eyes and stares at the metal collar wrapped around her left ankle. "Fart city, I always forget this damn thing." She yanks lightly on it, unwrapping it from the stool, and makes her way toward the small makeshift bathroom next to the bed. They gave her just enough chain for her to reach everything she might need.

It takes her a minute to understand it really is a baby crying, and not a wild animal somewhere outside.

"Maddy! Maddy! We have a surprise for you," Candy Sue calls out in a sing-song voice.

Maddy finishes her business and makes her way toward the voice. "Hello!" She steps back into the room.

Candy Sue motions toward the rocking chair seated next to a large table. "Have a seat, girl, this baby ain't gonna feed herself." Candy Sue stares down at the wriggling, crying bundle in her arms.

Maddy gasps and makes her way toward the chair. Milk pours

from her nipples. She rips her filthy blouse from her body. Snatching the baby from Candy Sue's arms, she cradles the small blonde haired child's face to a hardened nipple. It's almost too large for the baby's mouth, but Maddy squirts milk into the baby's open mouth.

Seconds later, the baby latches onto the nipple with hunger and longing. Maddy and the baby heave sighs of contentment. "There you go, sweet baby. Mama got plenty of milk. Suck away. We're gonna make you big and strong." Maddy pulls the blanket off the little girl's body, giving her a quick once over.

The baby snuggles closer to Maddy's breast, gulping down the warm milk.

Five fingers on each hand, face appears normal. *Why bring me the baby? Why? She's so beautiful. Oh God, please don't say they stole her. Please say they didn't.*

"She's perfect, isn't she?" Candy Sue takes a seat on the bed.

"She's the most beautiful baby girl I have ever seen. What's her name?" Maddy rubs her hand over the infant's head, cradling her closer.

"You can name her anything you like. She's yours."

"I don't understand." Maddy stares back at Candy Sue.

"Her mother was killed a few weeks ago. Well, killed is pretty harsh. She died in childbirth. We've been trying to feed her formula, but she has been vomiting it and everything else back up. Strangest thing we ever saw. Then a deal for you came along and we knew we had to take it."

Maddy glares at the other woman. She stops rocking. She cuddles the child closer, feeling the baby's heartbeat against her chest. "You knew about my past long before you snagged me at that lesbian bar in Miami. Long

113

before you got me drunk and asked me all about my family and me. Drunk. I spilled about growing up in an orphanage. How the priest and nuns sexually abused me. You already knew the story, didn't you?" Tears well up in Maddy's eyes, she struggles to keep them at bay. *How can I tell them now that I have no desire to leave? They will never believe me. Wait, she said they bought me? What the hell?* "What the hell are you talking about?"

"Oh, it ain't what you think. At first it was bad news for you. We originally wanted a sex slave. Someone we could sell out to the locals. They really like fucking up young girls like you but then Ole Mickey and I took a liking to you. We knew the baby would really love you and need you so … here you is. She's Ole Mickey's daughter, and I reckon from the sight of her, she turned out better looking than Ole Mickey."

Maddy nods. Lifting the baby from the breast, Maddy places the baby girl over her shoulder and pats lightly.

The baby lets out a hearty burp. One … two … three.

"That's a good baby," Maddy coos, as she latches her on to the second breast and finally feels the letdown flow through it, releasing her from the intense pain. Sighing loudly, Maddy glances back over at Candy Sue before staring back at the baby. "Why me?" she whispers.

Maddy searches her mind for times when she might have let down her guard and given away too much information about herself. The boys as she refers to them, the couple she gave the baby to, wouldn't have done it. They were so helpful and happy when she placed the baby boy in their loving arms. She never saw anyone take such good care of a baby, especially men.

The only other person … her best friend but even she wasn't privilege to everything. *She was pretty nosy at times though. She had, no, correction … she has a drug problem. She never used in front of me but there were times when she came home pretty messed up. We were never lovers, just friends, so why me?* Even as the questions flow through her mind, Maddy knows Tommie betrayed her.

"I don't know. I do know that Ole Mickey likes you. There's only been one other woman who wasn't afraid of him. Only one other that didn't think having sex with him the most repulsive thing ever. We both knew you had to be the one."

"Who told you about me? Who did you buy me from?"

"It ain't that important. You like it here, don't you? I mean except for the chain thing, we treat you pretty good, don't we? You do well and that chain thing will disappear too. So why cry over spilled milk now?" Candy Sue grins and shrugs. Her fingers dig into the arms of the chairs, as her eyes search the rug.

Shaking her head and grinning, Maddy gazes into the scared woman's face. "No need to fret. I'm staying. Not because of the baby. Not because of the chain neither, but because for

116

the first time in a long time, I feel loved. I'm just curious is all. I have an idea who sold me. Just wanted to confirm it is all."

Candy Sue nods and makes eye contact with her new friend. "Let's say the names at the same time and see if it is who we know it to be."

Maddy nods.

"One, two, three … Tommie," they both blurt out at the same time.

+++

"Noah, what the hell? Did you buy out the stores?" Deborah asks, as she lets him and several young men enter the large foyer.

"Where do you need these?" the tall brunette asks.

"Just drop them there," Deborah points toward a space by the elevator doors.

Both men place the items on and around a small table. Noah follows suit.

Noah pulls two hundred dollar bills from his pocket, and hands one to each. "Thanks again, buddies. I'll call you if I need any more help."

Neither says a word as they get back on the elevator.

Deborah and Noah hug as he air kisses her cheeks.

"Where are our girls?" Noah gushes.

"We're right here." We enter the room, Baby Chanah cuddles gently against my body in the new baby sling. Glancing over at the table overloaded with gifts, I grin. "Really, boyfriend, did you think I was broke?" I giggle.

He grins. "Well, it isn't every day my favorite girl reappears after disappearing for over a year. Then you bring a baby in tow. I'm so glad to see you." He races to my side and wraps his arms around me, holding me tightly against his body ever mindful of the little one between us. "Wow, motherhood really treats you well."

Shrugging and giggling, I lean upward to kiss him on the cheek. "It helps to have an expert helping me."

We make our way toward the living room and settle in.

"Let me make us some tea and plate up this food." Deborah picks up the bags from Zabars and makes her way toward the kitchen.

"Sweetie?" Noah takes a seat next to me.

I frown. I don't remember ever seeing this much concern on Noah's face before.

His dark eyebrows are knit together, and the laugh lines around his eyes deepen as he glances down at the baby.

"What is it?"

"Is Stan really gone?"

"Yes."

He gulps loudly and reaches to adjust his tie. It takes him several seconds to realize that he isn't wearing a tie. Small beads of sweat lace his forehead, and trickle down his neck into his shirt collar. "Stan was cheating on you."

"Yeah," I giggle, "and he and the bimbo were out on their asses the day I came home. Tell me something I don't know, Noah. Seriously, you're starting to scare me. You would think Stan had tried to get me killed, or was responsible for me getting attacked and then kidnapped."

Noah covers his face as soft sobs rack his body. "I don't know about that, but I did say something to the police about that when you were first taken. No, actually what I wanted to tell you is that he has a little drug problem. He and your so called literary agent are trying to screw you out of every penny you had even before you disappeared."

CHAPTER EIGHTEEN

Staring into Noah's eyes, I barely hear the words as he repeats them. *He and your so called literary agent … it all makes sense now. That's why she was calling and giving me a hard time about not having Stan in on any of my book deals. When I had disappeared I had already limited the funds Stan could receive from any of my accounts. If I died, he would still not receive the small fortune I had achieved.*

"Sweetie, are you all right?"

I feel the blood drain from my face as my heart races in my chest. I try to inhale but the oxygen strangles in the back of my nose and throat, never reaching my lungs. I cough and gasp. Tears sting my eyes, I reach for support but grasp air as everything goes black.

"Shoshana, Shoshana," the voices call out.

"I, uh … " I reach out and feel hands gather me up. Arms wrap around me, and it takes a minute for me to catch a hint of Noah's cologne. Opening my eyes, I hear the baby crying in the background. "I'm coming, baby girl."

"It's okay, sweetie. I have her." Deborah makes her way toward me so I can see her comfort Chanah. She coos sweetly to her.

I'm glad to see Chanah is okay. "I … I'm sorry. I think maybe I knew this all along but to hear it out loud. That's why I was checking out houses, I think." I gulp loudly and stare at my feet. My head still spins, as I lie back against the pillows.

"What were you going to do with the Penthouse? Give it to that asshole?" Deborah carries the baby back to the couch.

Shaking my head, I inhale deeply. The air feels cool against my nostrils. Taking several more breaths, I nod and reach out my arms toward her.

"Are you sure?" Deborah cuddles the baby closer to her breast. "You're not dizzy? You're not going to pass out, are you?"

"I'm okay. I'll lean back against the couch. You two are right here. I'm so sorry … I didn't mean to scare you." I can't take my eyes off of the shaking hands of my sister, as she hands over the baby. "Besides," I giggle, "I thought we were supposed to be eating some fabulous food from Zabar's."

Baby Chanah coos as she gazes up into my eyes. Her little lips curl up.

I reach for her hand and she clings to my finger. "You're so beautiful. Are you hungry?"

She yawns and stretches before closing her eyes once more and drifting back to sleep.

I sniff the top of her head before kissing it. Nothing like the sweet smell of a clean baby. Turning my attention back to Noah, I reach for him with my free hand. "I'm so sorry. I guess I knew something wasn't quite kosher, but they were so good at covering their tracks. I knew about the girlfriend, but my agent? What the hell? Can you tell me which came first … the agent or the drugs?"

Noah shakes his head. "Are you sure you want to know?"

"I've been in the dark for over a year. I'm going to have to go to court with this asshole, I need to know what I'm up against," I answer.

"I think it was about the same time that you disappeared that I learned about it. My guess is it has been going on for at least two. You might want to get tested for AIDS," he whispers the last sentence.

Shaking my head, I grin. "That ship sailed while I was back at the hospital. I was tested for everything. I guess Anastasia Esterhausen was also tested. We're all three very lucky, we caught nothing out there more than a pregnancy. Thank God."

Sighing loudly, Noah grins at me. "Thank God, indeed."

"Here comes the wonderful food." Deborah appears in the doorway with a large tray loaded with plates of food and glasses of sparkling grape juice.

Leaping to his feet, Noah races toward Deborah and takes the tray. He carries it to the large coffee table and places it in the middle.

Gazing around for the cat, I remind myself that there's no cat. "Where's Muffin? Or can I guess 'the pound'?" The last three words are barely audible.

"She's at my apartment," Noah chimes in.

Thank God. Thank God. Tears slide down both of my cheeks, I feel the damn ready to break.

+++

Cowering in the corner, Honey covers her eyes and sobs. Her lungs feel as if they will explode, as the pain in her face sears through her brain. Both eyes are swollen almost completely shut, and dried blood cakes cling to her skin from the bridge of her nose to the tip of her elfish chin.

Prying her eyes open, she tries to see over her fingertips. *Stan, where is Stan? What in the hell happened to me?* Her mind searches for the answers. The last thing she remembers before coming to this apartment was getting a text from Stan to come to this address. He left the keys in her purse.

What did that man do to my beautiful straight white teeth? Her hands automatically search the inside of her mouth. Blood clots layer the inside of her mouth, as well as drip down the back of her throat. It takes her a few seconds to realize that they are gone, all of them. *He took them. Oh God, he took them all, but why?*

I walked into the apartment and that man, she shudders, *he slammed me in the face with both fists. When I fell on the ground, he started kicking me in the stomach. He wouldn't stop no matter how many times I screamed. Oh God, it hurt so bad.*

Fresh tears form in her eyes as she remembers the look in his black eyes as he thrust the pliers into her mouth and ripped the first tooth from its socket. Everything goes black after that. *Oh God, what did I do to deserve this? Why? God. Why?* Her ears perk up as the sound of footsteps on hardwood reaches them.

She stiffens and draws her knees closer to her chest. She isn't even sure what room she's in. *How am I going to escape?*

"There you are, Honey," the giant of a man says, as he enters the room. He ducks under the doorframe to avoid getting a headache. His large arms and legs betray his hours at the gym, something he's as proud of as he is of his steroid usage. "I told you I'd be back." He grins.

"Please don't kill me," Honey begs, as she lays her cold naked body against the cool wooden floor.

Taking two strides, he's across the room and lifting the thin woman up with one hand. "Damn bitch, those tits are nice." His free hand grasps one and squeezes it with all his might. "These are real, I hope for your sake." He squeezes a little harder.

Honey's scream echoes off the closet wall.

"Are they real, or are they going to pop in my hands like water balloons. I'm hoping for the balloons myself, but breast meat does taste pretty good." He licks his lips.

"Please, oh God, please don't kill me. I'll do anything you want just don't kill me."

Sniggering loudly into her left ear, he slaps the back of her head with his fist. "Oh, I plan on doing what I want. When I'm done with you, you will wish you were dead. So you better hope I do kill you."

Stars float in front of her eyes, and the back of her head feels like it has been hit with a sledge hammer. *Oh God, please make him stop. I'll do anything. I'll stop having sex with Stan. I'll go back to West Virginia and go to work at the Dairy Delight, anything so I don't have to die. It would just kill mom and dad. Sister … surely sister will know I'm missing. She knows I was coming here. She'll tell the police. I left a message on her machine. Her cell. Where the hell is my cell? If I can just get to it.*

She gulps loudly as she tries to focus on the big man carrying her around the room. His large mitt is still squeezing the hell out of her left breast. "They aren't real," she whispers, as she hears a soft pop and a new sharp pain surges through her

chest. Silicon. They promised
this couldn't happen but then …
they weren't planning on anyone
using a vice grip on them either.

"Hot damn! I have a bingo!"
he yells at the top of his lungs.
He drops her on the large king
sized bed.

She lands on her back with a
dull thud and pop. New pain
forges its way up her spine.
"Ugh." She rolls over and
scrambles to her knees. Her hands
reach blindly for the edge of the
bed but each direction only
reveals more mattress.

He snickers and bounces onto
the bed. "I heard you suck real
good. At least that's what Stan
said."

Honey gasps and stops
moving. "What?"

"Oh, I think you heard me
the first time," he answers, as
he moves closer to her. "Open
your mouth wide for your big
surprise." His palms grind into
her knees, making her mouth pop

wide open. "Good girl. Here it comes."

She cringes and tries to pull back.

Wrapping his left hand around her hair, he pulls her closer to him and shoves a handful of whip cream into her open mouth.

Gasping, she closes her mouth and lets the sweet goodness slide down the back of her throat. It takes away the coppery taste of the blood and helps to wet her mouth. It tastes good.

"Okay, open your mouth for some more yummy cream," he says sweetly.

Honey closes her eyes and thrusts out her jaw, lips wide open.

He shoves his engorged penis between her lips and sighs.

Choking and gasping, Honey struggles to breathe. She tries to pull away, but his hands grip her ears, yanking her back and forth. "That's it. Stan is right, take those fucking teeth out and you can do all kinds of crap with a human mouth."

Oh God, no, Stan, why? Why would you do this to me? I love you, Stan, I love you.

CHAPTER NINETEEN

Staring at the paperwork, I cringe. "So basically Stan is saying that he should get half of everything I own including the Penthouse, is that right?"

Deborah snickers. "You have your copy of the pre-nuptials, right?"

"Yes, several although I found one copy shredded." I giggle. "I guess that asshole forgot that not only did I give your husband a copy, but there are copies at several safety deposit boxes around town. I was rich before I met him. He was no slouch. He had money in the bank.

I guess whatever drug addiction he has gotten into has him making some really bad choices."

"Well, enough with the business." Deborah snatches the papers from my hand. "If I remember correctly you were going to do some serious writing today, young woman. You need to not worry about these things and take care of business. Write … write … write."

Deborah twirls around and heads out the door. "By the way, the baby is fine before you decide to check on her."

Sighing loudly, I stare at the blank screen. She's right, I know. Even in captivity I was writing. I reach for the book once more and stare into the crumpled, splattered pages. I could get off into what that might be splattered on it but decided not to.

Why can't I remember anything but what I see in dreams? What could have been so horrible that I repressed it? What? I pick up the disc the hospital gave me of the night I was abducted. No, that isn't right. The police gave it to me, detectives. One of them wants to reopen my case. The phone rings as I pick up one of their business cards.

Reaching for my cell, I put the card back down. "Hello."

"You fucking, lying cunt," Stan hisses.

"Stan?"

His voice is so gravelly I almost don't recognize it. He mumbles softly into the other end.

What in the world is going on with this crazy man? I truly think he has lost it. "I don't know why you're calling. I received your papers this morning. I don't know why you think I owe you, but I don't. I don't appreciate your language either."

"You are supposed to be dead!" He sobs softly. "People

who are kidnapped are usually killed. Why aren't you dead?"

"Stan, even if I were dead you still wouldn't get my money. Don't you remember that document you insisted we have when we got married? You so knew that your modeling slash acting career would make way more than my little stories. Yes, I will pay you whatever it says I should but after that … " I sigh. "You need to figure out how to deal with the mess you're in." I start to hang up but change my mind. Putting the phone down, I hit the speaker button. I grab up my small digital recorder and set it on record. I set it gently back on the desk.

"You lying piece of shit. You're the one who demanded I sign that rigged crap. I would have never signed it, but you said I should stop being such an asshole and sign. I can't believe I didn't vomit every time I had to stick my dick into you. You are a fucking piece of work."

Normally tears would be racing down my face and I would

be begging him to stop talking such craziness but not today. Today I want him to get as ugly as possible as a memory forges its way back up my memory trail. I shudder and slink back into the chair as if I might hide in its blackness.

***

Wrapping my arms around his waist, I pull Stan closer.

"What the hell do you want?" Grasping my wrists tightly, he squeezes with all his might, digging his nails into them.

"Ouch." I wince and pull back. We're in the kitchen.

He's pouring us glasses of wine. He finishes his task and grabs his glass up. He downs half of it before refilling, and heading toward the living room.

"What was that for?" I follow behind him.

"What?" He doesn't even look my way as he plops onto the couch. He downs the other half of the wine before picking up the remote control. "Bring me the bottle. Looks like it's going to be one of those nights."

"Get your own damn bottle and I don't know what the hell you're talking about 'one of those nights'." I storm toward the office. I make it three steps before he leaps off the couch and races toward me.

Grabbing my arm, he twirls me back around almost knocking me into the wall. "You aren't going anywhere until you get me that bottle."

"You're up. Get it yourself. I'm not your slave." I shove back with all my might.

He stumbles and lands on his backside. "Fucking bitch, I'll show you not to give me respect. You can talk shit all you want with your good for nothing shit ass family, but around me you will do what I ask. Get me the damn bottle." He balls up his right fist, and aims it for my face.

Shaking my head, I sigh. I've only seen him this stupid once and it was a long time ago. It wasn't me he was angry at. "You need to put that down before it gets you hurt."

＊

"Are you listening to me? Are you even listening to me?" the voice on the telephone screams, bringing me back to the present.

"Huh?" I whisper.

"You stupid fucking bitch. You will give me twenty million and half of everything you earn from now on, or your year in Hell will seem like Heaven in comparison." Click and he's gone.

Smirking at the screen, I push the stop button on the recorder. Yeah, now I remember why I was going to look at the house. He tried to hit me. I let the rest of the scene play out in my brain.

＊

His fist flies toward my
face and I throw up my arm,
knocking it and him off balance.
Kicking with all my might, my
foot slams into the family
jewels.

"Ugh," he groans, as his
knees tremble and then buckle
beneath him. Grabbing his crotch
with both hands, he drops to his
knees.

My right knee slams into his
face.

His body drops to the floor.
Blood and boogers spatter the
hardwood floor as he scrambles to
stand, but lands flat on his ass.

"I guess you forgot I go to
exercise class three times a
week. Did I fail to mention it's
a Krav Magra class? Oops, sorry."
I step back, not wanting to get
blood and scum on my bare feet.

My heart races in my chest
as small beads of sweat pop out
on my forehead. *That's why the
cat is at Noah's, not because I
disappeared, but because I was
afraid Stan would hurt her. He*

139

tried to hurt me. I was going to give him the Penthouse and move to the 'burbs. I'll be damned if he gets it now, and I can't wait until the police hear this recording.

***

"Take a look at her," she whispers into his ear.

Gasping loudly, Stan turns his face away.

Reaching up, she slaps the back of his head with a loud swack. "I told you to look at the bitch. Look."

Tears sting his eyes as the shiny stars and moons float past his eyes, he shakes his head and turns his face back toward Honey. He barely recognizes the mutilated body lying on the floor. Honey's diamond tattoo on her ankle is the only identifying mark.

Loud sobs wrack his body, as he drops to his knees and cradles the young woman's body against his. He doesn't even care that he might be getting fingerprints on her. Her hands are gone as well as half her face and all her teeth. Two large gaping holes make up where her large plastic breasts used to sit, high and erect. Her belly is mush from the leaking implants. From the looks of it he guesses they were popped while they were still in her body.

She pulls back the blanket to reveal the woman's mutilated vagina and rectum. "I hear she was so so much fun that he almost didn't want to stop. Almost." She giggles and slaps the dead body knocking it askew.

"Why did you do this to her?" he gasps.

"I didn't. I told you not to move her ass into the apartment. I told you if you ever even thought about bringing her here I'd make a mess of her, but then I didn't have to, did I? I just had to tell your man about her, and he was cuming in his shorts before he even made eye contact." She rubs her crotch. "Oh God, I could cum now just thinking about all the shit he did with her. She fucking screamed and screamed your stupid bitch name."

"She was innocent," Stan whispers.

"She was a game. You played and you lost. Now she's shark bait like all the rest. You, Mother Fucker better keep your dick in your pants or this … " she points toward the body. "This can easily be you. I can't even imagine what he would do with your penis. Ooh … I'm guessing he would have some choice ideas for it."

"Please cover her up." He grabs the blanket up and wraps it back around his fallen lover's body." He holds it gently against her.

Cackling like a rooster, she rips the blanket from his hands and the body. "No, I'm not done yet. You know the ironic thing?"

Stan shakes his head. Never in his life had he encountered such sickness as her, and yet he finds himself so sexually attracted to it. More than even the drugs, but he never thought she would really come after his personal toy. Honey was so innocent. He leans down and kisses the top of the dead woman's forehead.

"The last words she heard before she died was that you, Stan the man, had sold her for a fix." She snickers and slaps the body again. Her grin reveals blindingly white teeth, she shoves the body towards him. "You have one more thing to do before we dump her ass. Drop your pants, I'm pretty sure she's got one more good fuck in her."

CHAPTER TWENTY

Staring at his penis, Stan shudders. Everywhere he looks, he sees Honey's face or rather what was left of her face. She had been one of the most beautiful women he had ever had the privilege of having sex with. *I can't believe she's dead. I can't believe they killed her. That woman is fucking nuts.*

Her blood and bodily fluids linger on his manhood, screaming at him to stop the pain, but he can't. "I think I really loved her," he whispers. He would never say that to that crazy woman, but he can honestly admit it now. In this room with no witnesses.

He gazes down at his naked body and reaches for his pants, but it is stuck to Honey's chest or what was left of her succulent breasts. He gasps and covers his face as he backs up against the doorway. *No, no, this is a dream. I'm going to go into the living room and the blood on my dick is going to disappear. I'm going to do a shot of dope and then come back here and take a nap. She won't be here. I just know it because this is all just a dream, and soon I'm going to wake up.*

He ambles into the living room thankful for the peace and quiet that being alone gives him. Dropping down onto the couch, he stares about the room as if he's seeing it for the first time.

A chandelier gives off enough light to brighten the whole room, even the small kitchen area. The room is almost bare except for two large black, soft leather overstuffed couches and two large glass top coffee tables. A bottle of water and a cup sits beside several spoons and a half a dozen syringes. Next to it is a sugar bowl, but he's pretty sure that roaches wouldn't want this kind of sugar.

He drops the baby scoop in, and pulls out a heaping spoonful. Placing the white powder into the closest spoon, he does this three times. Thinks about it for a second before scooping up another and tossing it into the spoon, he picks up a syringe and fills it with water. *Should I fill up two? Nah, I'm pretty sure this is pure enough to take just one.*

He watches the powder melt like snowflakes on a hot stove. He grunts loudly as he fills the syringe. The spoon is still full of thick liquid. He picks up the second syringe, and fills it as well.

Sighing loudly, he gazes around the room but everything is hazy, like a huge fog is filling it. Screams echo in his ears. "Help me, Stan, please help me!"

"I'm so sorry." He wraps the rubber tie-off around his arm. He usually doesn't tie off as his veins always seem to crave the drugs he puts into them, but today is different. Today he is feeding his and her need, and he wants to make sure he gets it right the first time.

Sliding the needle into the vein, he eyes the blood squirting back in and grins. He pushes in the plunger and releases the strap. His veins pulsate as the thick clear liquid rushes through the red. His heart skips several beats before blasting hard against his ribcage. Blood pulsates in his ears and eyes, as if they will be pushed off his head if he takes a deep enough breath. Tears fill his eyes and streak down his cheeks, as his breathing becomes shallow. His lungs pump hard against his heart, and he knows at any second they could both explode. They scream as loud as she screams in his muffled brain.

He grasps his ears, pushing them to their limits, trying to stop the noise and then suddenly there is nothing. No noise. No screams. Complete and utter silence. He picks up the next syringe in his trembling hands. He can barely focus as he brings the syringe up to his other arm. "I'm so sorry, Honey, I'm so sorry. I really do love you."

He gasps and moans softly as a soft white light reflects off the syringe hub. Red and white. He plunges in the syringe and listens intently as his heart skips a beat … a beat … two more skipped beats. Pain fills his chest as well as blood as his heart beats one more time before exploding into his chest.

CHAPTER TWENTY-ONE

Olivia and Kevin huddle together over the computer monitor.

"The damn thing worked pretty good yesterday," Kevin groans, as he gazes around the room to see if any of the computer nerds were close by. None.

Olivia shakes her head and frowns. "You big goof, it's unplugged." Olivia reaches down and plugs it back into the surge protector just as the screens pops back to life. A game of solitaire pops up on the screen. Olivia stares at her partner in amazement.

"Seriously? Solitaire? The way you were going on I thought you were working on something serious, and now I see it's just to make sure you win your game which by the way you have two moves and it's over." Olivia steps back to her chair and plops down in the soft leather, and returns her attention to the last of the paperwork for their last case. All she needs is to print and send to the chief for signatures.

Olivia eyes Captain McAfee as he makes his way from his office. His crew cut betrays his years of military service before coming to the NYPD. It no doubtable helped him with the transition to civilian life. "Olivia, you still all caught up in that Shoshana Meyers case?" He takes a seat on the edge of her desk and hands her a sheet.

"I just want to know who was involved with the kidnapping. I get the feeling that since she's been back we've been too busy with other cases to really grill her," Olivia answers. "Who the hell questioned her husband when she disappeared? We really need to get him in here and have a nice little discussion with him." The smirk on her face doesn't hide the disgust in her heart about the case.

"Well, it will be difficult to question him now, he's dead.

They found him about an hour ago. I want you to go and absorb before they move the bodies." Captain McAfee hands her the paper.

Leaping to her feet, she reaches for her cell and slides it into her pocket. "Let's roll, Solitaire man." Olivia pushes past the Captain.

"What does that mean?" Captain McAfee stands and stares at Kevin.

Kevin clicks off the screen and rises to his feet. "You know women. They ain't happy unless they got ya a nice snazzy nickname. Gotta go, boss."

Ten minutes later, Kevin and Olivia reach the apartment.

"What do you see?" Olivia takes in the neighborhood and sighs.

"We're only about ten blocks from her place."

Olivia nods and makes her way toward a uniformed female

cop. "Have they taken the bodies?"

Shaking her head, she points toward the ambulance. "No, they've been waiting on you two. You had breakfast?"

"No, why?"

"Cause what you're gonna see up there is gonna make you lose it." She sighs and heads off toward another officer. "I've been on this job for over twenty years. I've seen a lot of bad shit in my day but nothing like that. That is some pretty sick shit."

Olivia sighs and makes her way toward the elevator.

Neither say a word as they reach the apartment.

Olivia pulls a pair of rubber gloves from her pocket, as another uniformed officer points them in the direction of the first body. They don't usually work homicide cases. They usually work up missing persons cases where if there is a murder it gets kicked up to the next level. Olivia wonders why the captain decided to let them in on this case.

Both stop and stare in the doorway.

Tears fill Olivia's eyes, she swipes them away with the back of her jacket. She has only seen a half a dozen dead bodies in real life. Those were gunshot wounds but this … this is something different. This is even more gruesome than the ones she has seen on television. She races toward the woman's body, and drops to her knees, careful not to touch anything crime scene related.

Next to the mutilated body lies the young woman's heart. Several bites are missing.

"As far as we can tell it is a murder/suicide. Stan Marstonville is the suicide." The young male cop leans against the doorjamb.

Staring at the beat cop, Olivia bites her tongue to keep

the bile back down her throat. It churns several times but stays down. "What the hell are you talking about? A suicide? Is there a note? Where the hell is Marstonville?"

The man in blue shakes his head. "No, there isn't any note, but there's a butt load of coke and heroin in there. He has a syringe hanging from his arm."

Olivia jumps up and dashes to the living room.

Stan's naked body is lying on the couch. Dried blood is caked around his nose and mouth as well as his penis. His eyes are still open and staring blankly, a light film covers them. His mouth is open as if he's going to speak at any moment but for once in his life, he is silent.

Olivia and Kevin stroll around the room, moving items as needed.

Olivia eyes a lipstick resting under the curtain. Leaning down, she picks it up and eyes it. Dark purple. "Did we find a purse for the woman?"

Sighing loudly, the young man enters the room. "No, no purse. The weird thing is that unless his pants are under all that gore in the other room, we didn't find any clothes either."

"We went over everything. There's not even a weapon," a young blonde female cop voices as she enters the room.

Olivia nods toward her. "If he killed her and then killed himself, where are her missing parts? She has no fingers. Her face and teeth are gone. What the hell happened here? How could he do all of this and then kill himself?"

"Maybe," Kevin steps between the two women, "maybe he tossed the stuff and then came back here and overdosed."

Sighing loudly, Olivia shakes her head. "There are no clothes for either of them. What did he do? Walk to the incinerator buck naked and then come back here and overdose? And nobody saw him? That doesn't make any sense."

+++

Noah grabs the diaper bag and slings it over his shoulder.

I stop in the foyer and stare down into the car seat. I grin at the beautiful baby cooing back at me. She's so beautiful. Every day I look at her and can't believe she's mine.

"Do we have everything?" Deborah asks, as she checks the diaper bag.

"Oy," Noah chuckles, "if we get anymore things we will have to rent a station wagon."

"Well, I want to make sure we have everything we need," I answer. "It isn't every day that I have a baby naming with my baby."

Deborah sighs. "It will be all right."

My heart skips a beat as it drops into my belly. "What about food? Are you sure the caterers set everything up?"

"Silly, would I let you down? It has all been taken care of. There is enough food there to feed an army," Noah answers.

"No, no, you wouldn't let me down. If I know Zabars, they went way out of their way to make everything perfect," I answer.

The phone rings just as the elevator dings.

"Do you want me to answer it?" Deborah asks, heading toward the small table where an extension is kept.

"No, whatever it is, I don't want to deal with it. It's probably just the Rabbi's secretary making sure we're going to be there on time."

Deborah nods.

"Either that or the caterer wants to make sure you don't forget the check."

"I paid by credit card earlier today," I answer.

We make our way down to the rental car, and are on our way to the synagogue. In all my life I would never have thought it possible that I should be going to my own baby's naming.

CHAPTER TWENTY-TWO

"You aren't going to let this one go, are you?" Kevin asks, as they get on the elevator.

Olivia shakes her head. She's angry. Bile rises up the back of her throat, Olivia wishes she had eaten breakfast this morning. She'd rather taste regurgitated egg sandwich rather than the burning yellow juice. The woman's mutilated body floats before her eyes and she gasps. "He didn't do it."

"How can you say that?" Kevin asks.

"For one thing, where was the evidence? Yes, we have two bodies, but that woman was missing half her face, her fingertips, her breast implants and half her vagina."

"Not to mention her heart lying on the floor."

Olivia sneers at him. "With two bite marks, I might add. That alone will tell us if he was alone or had help. From what I could tell the bite marks won't match. Another thing that bothers me," Olivia begins.

"You mean other than we can't string this guy up now for the disappearance of his wife?" Kevin answers.

Olivia shakes her head and sighs. Sometimes her partner disgusts her. *That's it, freezer boy, nothing like your snide comments to bring me back to reality, but then you did work homicide for ten years before you came here. I just wish you had learned something except cynicism while you were there.* "And another thing … the syringe in his arm."

"What about it?"

"There was no blood in the hub."

"So, that doesn't mean anything. God knows … maybe he didn't hit a vein that time. Or maybe the drug was so pure that it dissolved it."

"Do you know how idiotic that sounds? First of all, there were three used syringes including the one in his arm. The first two still had a tiniest drop of blood still in them. Either in the needle or in the hub. Damn, the plunger would still have a tinge but not that one in his arm. No sir, that damn thing was placed in his arm after his death."

"Can we at least agree that he died of an overdose?"

Olivia shakes her head once more. "No, according to the coroner he died of a massive heart attack that caused his heart to explode. Yes, he probably had the heart attack due to the drugs, but it all goes together somehow. Did you see the test they did on the drugs? Pure heroin and cocaine. They'll run a full report on it but damn … when they showed me the results I was shocked."

Kevin nods. "I know. I talked to some of my connects in DEA and they said they hadn't seen that pure in a long time. This guy must have had big bucks and great helpers."

"Which goes back to Shoshana Meyers, she has that kind of money. I seriously doubt that she has any drug connections but she has two books on the bestseller list right now. She went viral when she disappeared and now that she's back, it's like a frigging resurrection. Even stuff she put out twenty years ago are selling out. Everyone wants to know where she has been and what happened."

Kevin smirks toward his partner. "And that includes us."

+++

"Did you take care of everything?" the gravelly voice asks. He takes a long drag off the Cuban and blows out several perfect smoke rings before grinning at Mary Elizabeth.

"Maybe with Stan out of the way she'll be more likely to open her wallet back up to me. I'm getting new monies from her oldies."

"And so is she. She wouldn't even be on top if she hadn't disappeared for a little while. I guess it's probably a good thing we didn't kill her off."

Mary Elizabeth snags the cigar from his hand and takes a small puff of her own. It's sweet taste coats her mouth and she inhales the smoke like it's oxygen.

"You taste pretty damn good, don't you?"

She winks in his direction as she takes another puff before handing it back to him. "Any time, baby, any time."

"It seems that our mountain folk are quite pleased with their replacement. May need to take a trip just to be sure. Seems like we need to go to plan C, but right now you need to go to Plan D as I think that Viagra has finally set in." Placing the cigar in its holder on the large dark mahogany desk, he leans back in his plush, black leather swivel chair. He pulls back his tie and begins to unzip his pants. The sound echoes off the solid cement walls.

She's down on her knees before the music stops.

Grasping her hair and pulling her face toward him, he whispers into her ear. "What do you want to do, bitch?" He nips at the top of her ear and licks up the blood as it trickles down her cheek.

She gasps and moans. "I want to suck your big powerful cock. Please sir, please let me suck your big powerful cock."

+++

Picking up the baby, Maddy takes her usual seat in the rocking chair. "Okay, baby girl. Sounds like you might be pretty hungry. Or is it ugly hungry?"She giggles. "Either way you are a very hungry little girl."

The baby latches on and sighs contentedly.

Maddy reaches for the bottle of water. She stares over at the six cases in the corner, and wonders for the thousandth time why they insist she drink bottled water only. She's surprised they don't demand she bathe in it, but then they probably don't think about that aspect. She giggles. They probably get their Saturday night baths.

"Hello," Candy Sue calls out as she enters the room.

Maddy nods in Candy Sue's direction, before turning her attention back to the baby. "Hey."

"Is she hungry again?" Candy Sue asks, as makes her way toward the kitchen area to prepare lunch. "I swear that little girl has tripled in size."

They both smiggle toward the baby.

"You know at some point you're going to have to name that little girl."

Maddy rubs the top of the little girl's head, sniffs it and grins. "I just don't know what to name her. She's so beautiful. Tell me about her mother. What was her name? Was she beautiful?"

Glancing around the room, Candy Sue listens intently. She steps over to the window and stares out. She watches as Ole Mickey strolls toward the wood pile with his double edged axe. "She was so beautiful. She was probably the prettiest girl from these parts in ages. Probably because her folks went to the city to live right after she was born. They came back a few years ago after she graduated from high school."

"Mickey really is the father, isn't he? I mean I know

that's what you told me, but she is so gorgeous." Maddy kisses the top of the baby's head again, and snuggles her closer.

"Yes, he is. Yeah, her mother did die in childbirth. She was a little thing. It's surprising that the baby lived. It was horrible. She screamed and screamed. The ole town doc, God, he must be a hundred if he's a day. Anyways, he came and he had to cut her open 'cause there wasn't time to get her to the hospital. The top of the baby's head was stuck in the hole. The cord was wrapped around her little neck and big body." Candy Sue shakes her head. "She weighed close to two sacks of potatoes. Then when we had trouble feeding her, she lost way too much weight."

"Either way, I love her," Maddy snuggles the baby closer to her.

CHAPTER TWENTY-THREE

Standing on the Bimah, I hold my baby against my breast. Even with all the accomplishments in my life, I could never feel prouder than I do at this moment. Tears fill my eyes, I barely see the people in the seats or my sister and her family.

Deborah leans into my back. "Are you all right?" she whispers so softly I almost miss her over my own loud racing heart.

I nod despite the nausea I feel creeping up the back of my throat. I search the audience, and not a single empty seat do I see. *Do I know all these people? Apparently I do, or at least they know me. I'm so happy, so why is this scary?* I inhale deeply and turn my attention back to the rabbi.

She grins at me, tears streak down her cheeks, and she does nothing to remove them. Her red cheeks betray her happiness as she beams at me and the baby.

"I feel like the luckiest woman in the world. For years I prayed with this woman as much or as many times as Hannah prayed with the priests in the days of old. I'm reminded of the High Holy Day sermons I work so hard on. The irony is that this little girl's name is Chanah. May her heart always be full and ready to serve as however blessed be should wish her to serve.

Today we welcome our newest member of the tribe …. Eliyah Chanah is her Hebrew name after her maternal grandmother who most of us knew and loved well. Eliyah Chanah will take her place amongst us and I pray that she never forgets her humble beginnings."

+++

Noah pushes the stroller as if he's an expert.

"Did you see that crowd?" Deborah asks, as we make our way toward the reception area.

I nod as I search for my best friend. We have spoken

167

briefly since my return to civilization. She had been out of the country and incommunicado at the time. Emily Greene, Bernadette and Sarah race toward me. They hug me tightly, tears streaming down their faces.

"Guys, why do I get the feeling I fell into the ocean?" I giggle. "Everywhere I go there's somebody showering me with the tears."

Sarah squeezes my arm and pulls me away from the center of the crowd. "I can't believe that when I finally take a few days off from looking for you, you show up. How the hell could you be right under my nose the whole time?" She snickers and kisses my cheek.

I kiss hers back and shrug. "You got me. I'm just glad to be here."

Sarah makes her way toward the baby. "I told you it was all Stan all along. Men. So willing to go to a movie house with a group of strangers and spill their seed everywhere, but not many of 'em can do it at the damn doctor's office."

Everyone cracks up.

"That's my Sarah, always willing to say exactly what's on her mind. You're so silly. Let's get something to eat, I'm starving." I nod toward the caterers who are already serving hungry guests a lovely brunch.

+++

"Did you get everything?" I ask as I click the baby carrier into the stroller, and reach for my purse.

"I've got it," Deborah holds it up for me to view.

"I've got the diaper bag." Sarah makes her way toward me.

"Don't worry about it," Noah voices, as he shuts the doors. "We can come back to get the rest of the goodies when you are safe inside." He nods toward the doorman who stands ready.

"Okay." A cold shiver races up and down my spine, and my heart skips a beat. I glance around to see if there is a breeze, but everything is still but the loud beating of my heart. Something is wrong. I don't know how I know, but I do.

As we step into the lobby, I catch sight of the two detectives. I've never met them, but I'm pretty sure I've seen them before.

"Shoshanah Meyers?" the tall brunette woman asks, as she and the big man with her make their way toward us.

"I paid my bills, I swear," I say with a giggle. "Just kidding. You two look like detectives."

"What do you want now?" Deborah steps between me and the detectives.

"Can we go up to your apartment?" the man asks, as he steps toward the elevators.

"Sure, I can't guarantee it isn't a mess but yeah, that's fine," I answer.

"What are you talking, mess?" Sarah snorts. "This woman cleans even when she has full time help and doesn't have to. I guarantee it's cleaner than my place."

"Or mine," the woman interjects.

"We'll see when we get inside, but honestly I'm pretty sure the NYPD has better things to do than inspect Manhattan apartments," Noah adds.

No one says a word, as we ride the elevator. Even Chanah is silent.

As we step into the foyer, I note all the gifts have been delivered and anxiously awaiting my attention. It'll have to go on the to-do list. I realize then that I haven't even asked for their names and badges. That's so not me even before the kidnapping.

"Can I offer you some coffee?" Deborah asks.

"I'm sure the officers would love some coffee," I tell her. "You are police, aren't you?"

Deborah races off toward the kitchen and the coffee maker.

"My name is Officer Olivia Lincoln, and this is Officer Kevin Mc Ginnis." She puts her hand out to me and I shake it.

The shiver races up and down my spine again and I shudder. "I'm Shoshana Meyers, please come in. Did you find my kidnappers?" I lead them into the living room.

They take the two chairs from the dining room table that was set out earlier when we were making baby naming plans.

"My sister Deborah just went into the kitchen. These are my friends, Noah and Sarah."

They both nod toward them.

"Actually," Olivia sighs, "we didn't come here with good

news. Your husband, Stan Marstonville was found dead earlier today."

"Oh my gosh," I gasp, as my hands cover my mouth. *Where is the baby?* My heart leaps into my throat, as I reach for my little girl in her corner. I need her in my arms. Although I have no love left for the vile, despicable piece of crap that I call Stan, I would have never wished him dead.

"Somebody catch him with his wife, and run over his creepy self?" Noah asks.

"Actually, he overdosed," Kevin answers.

"Drugs?" I gasp. This is a man who would barely take an aspirin when he had a headache and now they say he is dead of an overdose. How? Shaking my head, I reach for Sarah.

"Yeah, girl, he was starting up pretty good before you disappeared. I guess you didn't notice because you were finishing a book and a book tour at the time. He actually tried to borrow money from me. He told me you had put him on a five hundred dollar a month allowance." Sarah squeezes my hands.

I shake my head. "You know better than that."

"I made sure his account had three thousand a month as per you guys' agreement. I've been doing it ever since, even while you were gone. I paid all the bills just as if you were here, so that he didn't have to use any of his money to pay the bills. I didn't want him trying to say you owed him," Noah voices, forgetting for a moment that two detectives sit in here with us.

I sigh and shake my head. "I don't get it. Why would he use drugs?"
"What did he do for a living?" Kevin asks.

"He was a model," I answer.

"He was a freeloader. You two ever check into where he was when she was being beaten half to death or kidnapped from the hospital? The detectives before

174

you sure seemed to think ole Stan was innocent," Deborah says, as she enters the room with a tray full of coffee cups.

"I don't really know what happened with the other detectives. They gave us the case today when Stan was found," Kevin answers.

"You won't have to identify the body because his family was able to come," Olivia states.

I sigh. The last thing I really want to do is identify his body. I gaze over at the detectives and frown. Both are sweating despite the coolness of the room.

Pulling a white handkerchief from his pocket, Kevin swipes it across his forehead.

Both reach for cups and decline cream and sugar.

"We haven't found your kidnappers, but we are on your case. I'm going to leave you a card. If you think of anything, please feel free to call."

Standing, Olivia hands back her cup to Deborah.

Deborah leaps to her feet and takes the cup back to the tray set on the coffee table.

"That would be great. I apologize if I seem a little spacey. We had the baby naming today and I am feeling a little overwhelmed." I stand as well as everyone else.

"No need to get up, I'm sure your sister can let us out." Kevin hands her a card, and he and Olivia make their way toward the elevator.

Deborah is right on their tails.

No one says a word as we all listen for the dings of the elevator, both coming and going.

Deborah makes her way back into the living room.

"Wow," I gasp.

Everyone's eyes are on me. I gaze around the room. I don't

know whether to cry or shout. Glancing down at the baby, I just shake my head. "I can't believe it. I really didn't wish him dead, but I sure as hell am not sad he is gone."

CHAPTER TWENTY-FOUR

Easing back into the chair, I sigh. *Stan is dead. Oh my gosh, Stan is dead. I should call his family. They probably didn't even know we were separated.*

"Do you need anything?" Deborah asks, as she steps into the room.

Glancing her way, I shake my head. "I was just wondering if Stan has contacted his family since we separated. If not they're probably wondering where I am."

"Knowing Stan, he didn't even tell them you were gone or had returned. You know them. They don't read the newspapers or watch the news."

"This is true. The last year that I was here they had become more isolated. I was worried about their mental status, but his brother and sister assured me that they were fine."

"Let me fix you a cup of tea, then you can get back to work, or maybe a nap. You aren't looking so good." Deborah squeezes my shoulder.

"Thanks, I probably do need a nap. I was so tired last night, but I just couldn't sleep. I just kept seeing Stan's face as he lies in a casket. I didn't want him to die, and according to the newspaper he was with her. I sure hope the police don't think I killed them." I shudder and swallow down the lump of fear that has been growing in the back of my throat since the detectives gave us the news.

"Now, you are just talking crazy." Deborah giggles.

Snickering softly, I grin back at her. "You know us writers, we think the world revolves around us. I know I didn't do it. I didn't even drive him to it. I'm just glad I have you and Noah and all the others to back me up because I get the feeling this is going to get quite messy for someone."

+++

"Olivia, are you gonna stare at that same screen all day, or get some real work done?" Kevin asks, as he leans over her shoulder and clicks the monitor power button off.

"Hey! I was studying that," Olivia wails.

"You're staring at a picture of a mutilated dead woman. You've been staring at her for over an hour now. What exactly do you think you're going to get from that?" Kevin takes his seat behind his own desk.

Olivia shrugs. "I was kind of hoping that maybe she would speak to me."

Kevin sniggers and leans back in his chair. "When that happens you better let me know so I can make sure to save you a room at Bellevue. I hear they have a special for jaded cops with a God complex."

Sneering at him, she flips the power button back on and the monitor pops back to life. The ringing phone makes her heart skip a beat. "Stanton here."

"Hey Ms. Marky Mark," the female voice answers.

"Hey, Carolyn, what you got for me today?" Olivia asks. Carolyn is one of the coroners. She's the only one Olivia allows to call her by the Mark Wahlberg reference. It started when Carolyn learned Olivia's middle name is Mark. It was supposed to be Marla, but someone couldn't read the handwriting, and she became Olivia Mark Stanton.

"I hear you and Kevin are working the Marstonville case."

"We are, what you got for us?" Olivia grabs a pen and a pad, and leans against the desk.

"I need you two to come here. This is too big for you to hear over the phone. You got time right now?"

"I think I can pull solitaire man away from the computer for five." Olivia giggles.

"I'll be here." Click.

"Let's go see Ms. Carolyn." Olivia snags up her pad and pen, and stuffs them into her backpack purse.

"Now we're talking." Kevin grins as he pulls a small mirror from his desk and checks his receding hairline.

"Oh you," she giggles, and slaps his arm with her bag.

"Ouch! Help! Police! I'm being sexually harassed," Kevin calls out.

No one in the busy precinct glances their way.

"See what happens when you holler wolf so many times. You could be choking on a donut in the middle of the room, and they would probably think that you were playing with charades." Olivia heads toward the elevator.

"Funny, very funny."

They reach the coroner's office fifteen minutes later.

"What you got for us, Carolyn?" Olivia asks, as they enter the door.

"Well hello to you too." Carolyn grins from her desk in the corner. She hops up from her chair and slips the hair tie from her wrist. Pulling back her thick blonde curls, she makes a tight bun at the nape of her neck.

Kevin eyes her neck and gulps. "Hello."

"What you got for us?" Olivia pulls out her pad and pen.

"I have Stan on the slab."
She points toward the sheet
covered body on the metal
examination table.

All three step toward it.

"We know he died of a heart
attack, so what else is new?"
Olivia asks.

Carolyn pulls down the
sheet. "I think there was someone
else in the room when he died. I
did bite markings from the heart.
I figured if it was your general
murder/suicide then he did all
that and bit the heart. Crazy as
that might seem. You get to see a
lot of crazy stuff in the
coroner's office." She giggles.

"So what is different here?"
Kevin asks, finally finding his
voice.

"There are two bites missing
from the heart. One bite is
Stan's but the other is not. The
weird part is that I expected to
find the heart piece still in his
stomach but it wasn't. It's as if
he took the bite and then spit it
out. His stomach had been empty

for some time, but I suspect with the type of drugs he was doing that it had been a while since he'd been able to eat."

"What about the tox screen on the needles?" Kevin asks.

"Two needles tested positive for cocaine and heroin. The third syringe they found in his arm didn't even have blood in it. Somebody put that needle in after he was dead. The fact is there hasn't been anything in that syringe, ever. It was brand spanking new." She sighs.

"But we know he died of an overdose," Olivia insists.

"No, he died when his heart exploded. Yeah, drugs were probably the cause but the official cause of death is a massive heart attack. Yes, the drug overdose will be included before you get your hackles up," Carolyn points toward the bruises along Stan's neck and shoulders.

"That's one of those mysteries I can't figure out." She steps toward the second metal table where Honey's body lies.

"If you look over at her," she lifts the sheet, "she has the same set of bruises on her."

Olivia and Kevin stare at the markings along the woman's neck.

"Did you find any drugs in her system?" Kevin asks.

"No, there wasn't even an aspirin in her system but I did find something else. She was pregnant. Maybe six weeks. Another thing I found out about her is that there was two, maybe three different sets of DNA in what was once a woman's vagina. I've been trying to be thorough with a throat swab as well."

"I have to know," Olivia begins.

"Which came first?" Carolyn adds.

Olivia nods.

"Her torture came first. She was still alive, just barely, but still alive when the sick son of a bitch ripped out her heart."

"Do you think he knew this?" Kevin asks.

"Of course that is probably neither here nor there, but I found that significant considering that I was shocked when I saw that none of her other pieces and parts were recovered."

"Someone else was in the room. So we have an open investigation," Olivia voices.

Kevin nods.

"You most definitely do," Carolyn answers, "and the sooner you can get the sick bastard off the streets who did this, the easier I will rest."

Kevin chuckles. "At least until the next sick asshole shows up anyway."

+++

Slipping her hands between her thighs, Mary Elizabeth gasps as they reach their mark. "Oh God, it felt so good watching him fuck that dead body. The look on his face was priceless." *Oh God,*

I wish I was sitting in that room all over again. He came so hard I thought he was going to blow the top of her head off, at least what was left of her head.

"You were right, Honey was lots of fun." The low male voice says from behind.

"I hadn't had that much fun since …" Mary Elizabeth stops moving her hands for a minute, " … oh yeah, since you and I were just starting out. Terrorizing that young girl in college."

"Fucking bitch had it coming. Wearing those tight shorts, flashing her tits all the time. She was rubbing them against you every time she had a chance."

She squeals and shudders. "How could you fuck her and pull her teeth at the same time?"

"I don't know." He pulls some ropes from a backpack. "You ever hear of the Sondercommando?"

"That's some World War II crap, isn't it?" she asks,

removing her hands from under her skirt and sighing loudly.

"Uh huh." He nods toward the large wooden table.

She stands and makes her way toward it. She wishes she had a syringe in her hands. A good shot of dope would go nicely right about now.

"Well, when Hitler and his crew decided to go into their final solution they knew they needed to use the ultimate in psych warfare."

"What does that mean?" She pulls down her tight skirt and drops it on the floor.

"They wanted them to think they were going to take showers, right?"

"Huh?" Mary Elizabeth reaches for her skirt.

Grasping the top of her thigh, he squeezes tightly.

"That's it baby, fuck me up. Hurt me, baby, make me come all over your big dick."

He chuckles and sighs. "Anyway, they made a group of Jewish men called sondercommandos take the Jews to the showers. They were there while they undressed and prepared to take a shower after the long rides on the train."

"Yeah, yeah, I get it. They used Jews so the Jews being killed wouldn't recognize the danger. Millions of people went to their deaths thinking they were just taking showers." She reaches into his pants and feels his hardness in her hands. Her heart skips a beat as her mouth waters, and she drops to her knees. She releases it before engulfing his maleness into her waiting mouth and begins sucking on it like a lollipop.

His hands wrap around her hair and he shoves her down on him. "That's right, you dumb cunt. I'm trying to tell you something that might save your life, but you'll never hear it.

189

You'll probably die this way, getting fucked every which way but loose."

CHAPTER TWENTY-FIVE

Olivia and Kevin glance up and down the block, watching all the people rushing about.

Monday mornings are always busy, no matter what street a person is on.

"Is this is?" Kevin asks.

Staring down at the six layers of police tape lying on the ground close to the Harlem's alley's entrance, Olivia nods. "It has to be it. I came here right after it happened but it looks different somehow."

They walk up the way.

Olivia shakes her head. "No, it's pretty much the same as it was then. I remember thinking at the time I wonder why the trash hasn't been picked up here."

Kevin nods. "I asked about that before we came. The sanitation people said they've accidentally picked up three hobos in the dumpsters here. No one's been killed so far, but I think they're afraid that someday someone will get hurt."

"I'm guessing they want someone to run interference first, right?"

Kevin chuckles.

Olivia edges her way toward the spot where Shoshana gave birth. Soft moaning stops her in her tracks. Putting up her hand to Kevin, she listens intently.

Nothing.

Olivia slips a pair of gloves from her pocket and dons them. She picks up several dried, bloody cloths and tosses them. They look old, almost ancient.

Amongst the old clothes and trash are syringes and broken crack pipes. A junkie's delight.

Soft moaning stops both of them.

"Do you hear that?" Olivia glances back at her partner.

"To tell you the truth I didn't know if it was your stomach or mine. When are we going to get some lunch?" Kevin asks.

"I think it's coming from over there." She races toward a taller pile of old clothes and trash bags.

Both grab and chunk bags of garbage, rags, empty bottles and empty fast food containers.

"Oh my gosh," Olivia gasps, as she reaches in and grabs an arm.

Seconds later, they pull the woman's body from the rest of the pile, and lay her on a mattress of discarded clothes.

Kevin flips open his phone and dials 911 before either can say a word.

Olivia feels for a pulse, as she feels for the soft air puffs blowing from the woman's lips.

The woman's naked body is caked in dried blood. Her face is swollen beyond recognition and blood pools around her lips drifting down her chin. Her eyes are just barely slits, letting only a little light filter through. "Oh Gawd, no!" She screams, and slaps Olivia's hands away.

"It's all right," Olivia grabs the woman's wrists. "We're the police. We're here to help you."

The woman's eyes widen and she screams again. It echoes off the brick walls."No, get away from me. They'll kill me if you help me."

"We can help you," Olivia insists.

The woman closes her eyes and screams louder.

Olivia glances down at the large T carved in the middle of the woman's body, swallowed up by the blood, and sighs softly. *I don't know for sure, but if I were a betting woman, I would bet this woman knows who was in the room when Stan was killed. Why do they keep picking on this alley? Oh no, Scooby Doo, looks like we just found another clue.*

+++

"What the hell do you mean, she just died?" Olivia asks.

"We had her in ICU. We had just given her two units of blood. She was stable. One of our other patients went into cardiac arrest. It took all of us to deal with it. By the time I got back to her, maybe fifteen minutes later, she was gone." She sighs. "I'm so sorry."

"Did they do a rape kit?"

The nurse nods.

"Okay, well at least that's a start." Olivia stares around the hallway. It's surprisingly quiet.

"Did we find out the woman's name?"

"Mary Elizabeth Harper. She was a literary agent."

"Oh, wow, was she Shoshana Meyers' literary agent? I sort of remember seeing her here when Shoshana was here with the baby. I just passed her in the hall. I saw her on television a few years ago. Believe me, two years ago that woman didn't look like she did before she died. Wow! What happened to her?" the nurse prattles on.

"That's what I'd like to know too," Olivia answers. "You said she came to visit Shoshana Meyers."

"Yeah, well, I don't know if she actually saw her. She stopped me on the elevator and asked me if I knew where she was. I told her. I didn't think anything of it as I knew the police were at her door. Nothing bad could happen. She told me thank you, but then she didn't get off at the maternity floor. Just when I was going to ask her about it, we were at my floor. My beeper went off, and I had to go. To tell you the truth, I had forgotten about it until now." The nurse shrugs.

"Do you have a card?" Olivia asks.

The nurse pulls a small pouch from her pocket. "We started giving these to the families a few years ago. That way they can just call me directly to ask questions about their loved ones. My name is Shirley Mc Entire."

Olivia pulls a card from her pocket and hands it to the nurse.

"I'll let you know if I hear of anything. I really want to help." Her beeper goes off and she dashes away.

"Hello," Olivia answers, as she answers her ringing cell.

"Your best buddy Carolyn here."

"I bet you are learning so much, aren't you?" Olivia snickers.

"Actually, I just received another body about an hour ago."

"Let me guess, Mary Elizabeth Harper."

"Are you reading my mind?" she giggles.

"I just got through talking to her ICU nurse."

"Well, girlfriend, come on down and I'll tell you the other good news."

Olivia clicks off and heads for the stairs. No time for elevators. Her mind races at the newest possibilities. "Hello, best friend," she says, as she enters the morgue.

"Well, hello to you too." Carolyn grins. She doesn't say a word. She points Olivia toward a slab and they move toward it.

Picking up a medium sized Ziplock evidence bag, she pulls the heart from the bag.

Each bite mark is tagged with a number.

Pointing toward the bite marked two, she reveals Mary Elizabeth's teeth in comparison with the indentations.

Gasping loudly, Olivia's thrilled that she isn't the one holding the heart. *Well, I'll be damned. Little Ms. Mary Elizabeth is not the sweet innocent business woman she has appeared to be all these years.* "Are you seeing a pattern here too?"

Carolyn chuckles. "I should be the detective on this one. There are just way too many co-incidences on these things. I just took a chance on checking the bite marks. I really figured I was pissing in the wind on this one. Speaking of pissing in the wind, where's your partner?"

"He had an emergency at home. I think one of his children

is sick. His wife is in surgery all day."

"Oh, yeah, she's Dr. Sanderson, isn't she? Yeah, I've seen her around the cafeteria before." She giggles. "That man is shameless, isn't he?"

Olivia grins. "He has his moments. He did finally agree with me that there are more involved than we first thought. The big question now is how far down the rabbit hole does this go, and whether or not we should take the blue pill or red pill."

+++

Picking up the address book, I search for Stan's parents' phone number. *I hope they didn't give the phone up. Ugh. Okay, woman, you have faced so many things, this is tiny in comparison.* Sighing loudly, I pause and stare at Chanah.

Chanah yawns and stretches. Her eyes smile at me.

"You're beautiful. So very beautiful. Mommy loves you."

Deborah steps into the room. "Is she awake?"

"Yeah, she's fine. I need to call Stan's parents."

"Are you really sure you want to do that?"

I nod. Picking up my cell, I dial their number. It rings several times before a soft female voice answers and I recognize it as Stan's sister Katie. "Katie?"

"Shoshana?"

"Yeah, Sweetie, it's me. I just wanted to call and let you know that I'm sorry about Stan."

"I wanted to be angry at you when Stan told me you kicked him out but I couldn't be. I hadn't talked to him in almost two years. Then out of the blue he calls me. He asked me for ten thousand dollars. I told him if he needed ten thousand dollars he should get a job. Did he tell you about the two modeling schools trying to head hunt him for work around here?" Katie asks.

"When did this happen?" *He never told me anything. Anything.* I sigh.

"Almost two years ago."

"He never mentioned it to me."

"I knew he wouldn't. He just kept saying that you needed to give him more money and if he had a mind, he might start selling some of your things."

"Why? What did he need that much money for? Everything was paid for. He had his own money, as well as the allowance he demanded. I still don't understand." I sigh. "Enough about Stan, how about your parents?"

This time it is her turn to sigh. "It's not good," she gasps. "I had to put both of them in a nursing home a couple of months ago. She has severe Alzheimer's, and he had a stroke about three months ago. I tried taking care of them here but it was impossible."

"I'm sorry to hear that," I whisper.

"I've talked it over with my brother and uncle. We're not even going to have a funeral. As soon as Stan's body is released we're going to have it cremated. We might do a memorial but not likely. Stan was pushing all of us away long before you came into the picture. He always thought he was better than us because of that damn modeling. As far as I can see that's what ruined him in the first place."

"I'm still sorry for your loss."

Katie sighs. "My biggest loss is my mom and dad. My mom was my best friend. Listen, I have your number. I promised the nurse I would come up and try to help Mom eat today. I'll give you a call if we decide to do anything else."

"Make sure to take care of yourself, okay?"

She giggles. "I'll try."

The soft click lets me know she is as quick with the disconnect as before. When I first met her I thought she was being rude. It took a while to realize she just didn't like to say good-bye. Glancing down at the area code it takes me a minute to fit it in, 304, West Virginia. *Aren't they in the Appalachians?*

CHAPTER TWENTY-SIX

Olivia smirks at her partner as she makes her way toward their desks.

"What are you grinning about, Ms. Cheshire Cat?"

"I know who was at the murder scene of Honey and Stan," she says with a deep sigh, as she slides into her chair.

"So I guess you were overly busy while I played mommy dearest," he answers.

"Something like that. I was just at the offices of Harper Literary Agency to inquire about the latest victim in this case."

"So let me guess, our little find died."

Olivia nods. "Yes, yes she did. Carolyn said she did a bite identification … "

Kevin throws up his hands. "Just the facts, ma'am."

"Okay, okay … the lady we found was Mary Elizabeth Harper. She was present when Honey was having her heart served as lunch. She was Shoshana's literary agent. You already know we found her in the same alley as the one where Shoshana was found."

Kevin nods. "Shit, are they still letting us work this case? Seriously, this sounds more like it needs to be stepped up to homicide."

This time it is Olivia's turn to nod. "The captain says it is ours unless the Feds get called. Right now we just have to get through this one."

He eyes her as her hands swiftly fly across her computer keyboard. "What else have you learned?"

"Ms. Harper and Shoshana … "
"… were on the outs. It figures."

"You don't think that Shoshana would come back and want revenge, do you?"

"Someone attacks me. Puts me in the hospital and then kidnaps me, making me disappear for over a year, I'm pretty sure if I ever came back I would feel a little vengeful too. You want to go back and talk to her, don't you?"

"I don't think she did it, but I get the feeling that she may be the next target," Olivia answers.

+++

Picking up a small picture frame, Katie stares down at the little boy and girl in it. She swipes the tears from her eyes. *Thank God Mom and Dad can't see this insanity. Damn, at least he didn't look like his girlfriend.* She sighs. "I know you're in on this nasty stuff with Shoshana. I don't know how but I know it well, and I'm going to get to the bottom of it, if it kills me."

+++

The buzzer rings, pulling me from my thoughts.

"I got it," Deborah calls out.

"Okay," I yell back, as I pull Chanah from one nipple, and latch her to the other one.

Deborah steps back into the living room. "It's those two detectives. I gave them the okay to come on up. I hope you're okay with that."

"That's great. Did they happen to mention why they are here?" Already my mind is whirling. What could they want? "Sister … "

"I'm already on the coffee." Deborah heads toward the kitchen.

A few minutes later the bell rings and Deborah races from the kitchen. She opens the elevator and allows Olivia and Kevin to enter.

"Hello, she's in the living room feeding the baby."

"Thank you," Olivia answers.

"Come on in," I holler, as I reach for a blanket to cover up. I pray modesty isn't important to them because if there is one thing I've learned since starting the breastfeeding road, it's that the blanket doesn't always stay up.

"Hello," Olivia and Kevin speak as they enter.

"Hello, have a seat. Deborah will be back with some coffee in a few minutes. I'm really surprised to see you too," I lie. *You want to know if I killed my husband, don't you?*

"Thank you," Kevin answers, as he glances down at the floor.

"So what brings you?" I ask with a sigh.

"We're concerned about you. We know there's a door man, and that you can't get to this floor without being allowed up, but so far three people that knew you and Stan are dead."

"Oh my God! You think they might try to hurt me and the baby?" I gasp.

"It would really help if you could remember more of what happened while you were gone. Maybe some of the faces of your abductors. Any details would help us greatly." Olivia takes a cup from the tray in Deborah's hands.

Kevin picks up a cup as well.

"To be honest, a part of me wishes I could completely forget that part of my life. At this moment, I just haven't been able to recall a thing. Believe me, I've tried." I hesitate. *Do I*

risk telling them about the book?
Or should I just assume the
drawings and writings are just my
wonderful imagination? Fear tugs
at my heart.

Deborah eyes me as she sets
the tray down on the coffee
table.

I shrug.

"Are you all right?" Olivia
asks.

"Who else has died?"

"Your agent, Mary Elizabeth
Harper," Kevin answers before
taking a long sip of coffee.

"When the hell did this
happen?" I snuggle the baby
closer to my bosom.

"They just released it to
the press this morning."

Shaking my head, I drop it
into my free hand.

"She was found in the same
alley where you gave birth. We
get the feeling there is some

sort of connection," Olivia remarks.

"Oh my goodness," Deborah gasps.

I sigh. My heart is in my throat. Tears burn my eyes but they refuse to leave them. I didn't hate her, I just didn't want to have her represent me anymore.

"I think you should tell them," Deborah voices, pulling me from my wonderful thoughts.

"Tell us what?" Kevin asks.

"When she came home from the hospital, she received a phone call from her agent. The woman demanded that she turn over half the take on the last book to Stan. By then she had already kicked Stan out."

Olivia and Kevin turn toward me.

"Is this true?" Kevin asks.

I feel my face heat up as my heart skips a beat. My palms

dampen instantly, and I swipe them on the back of the baby blanket. My brain runs crazy with ideas. If this were a horror movie, I'd probably be elbow deep in popcorn and soda, anxiously waiting for the answers.

"Yes, it is true." Glancing down at the baby, I smile as her lips curl up and release my nipple. I slide my top back over my breast

"She also has a recording of Stan attacking her verbally over money. They both seemed to want Shoshana's money. I'm no Sherlock Holmes, but I'm pretty sure those are clues to help you solve this mystery."

"Do you still have it?" Olivia asks.

I nod. "It's still in my office."

Before anyone can say anything, Deborah is up and back with the recorder. She hands it to Olivia who plays it.

No one says a word as the ranting begins and ends.

"I kept it because I figured I would need it for the nasty divorce. I guess I hadn't thought about it since." I stand and move toward the bassinet, my hands tremble as I lay the baby inside. Wrapping another blanket about her, I lean down and plant a kiss on her forehead.

"Yeah, I can understand why you would feel that way."

"I've contacted his sister. She isn't even going to have a service for him. He's been out of the limelight awhile so I don't even know if they will give him an honorable mention." I take my seat.

"You really don't watch television, do you?" Kevin asks.

Deborah giggles. "It's funny that you should say that. I remember when she watched a lot of television but not now. I think I've seen her watch a few movies since she's been back and that's it. It's sort of strange."

"He was given a lot of lip service this morning. One of those 'whatever happened to?' Sort of segments. He didn't fare well there either. They even mentioned you, but only because you two were married. They were all excited about a possibility of a book about your missing year," Kevin states.

"Is that a possibility?" Olivia asks.

I snicker and shake my head. "Yeah, I guess it will be when I finally recall everything. My publisher would love such a book. Fiction or non."

"Can I get you two some more coffee?" Deborah jumps up and heads for the kitchen for the pot even before they can answer.

"Please, please let us know anything you can. We really do believe that your life is in danger again which is why there will be around the clock police surveillance outside."

+++

Katie steps inside her parents' room. She half expects them to be in their beds but today they're sitting up in their wheelchairs.

Her dad smiles at her. "Hello, Katie baby. How are you doing on this fine Tuesday afternoon?"

Katie's mouth gapes open, as she gasps and tries to catch her breath. Her heart skips a beat, and tears fill her eyes. He hasn't spoken since the stroke. In fact, she has only seen a glossy look in his eyes as well, and now here he is … sitting in a chair and speaking.

"Ms. Katie bug," Mom calls out. "Is that you, Ms. Katie Bug?"

"Mom! Dad!" she races to their sides. Dropping to her knees, she reaches for their hands. "How are you doing today?"

"You are so beautiful today," Mom voices.

"Thank you."

The nurse pops her head in the doorway and grins. "I was hoping you would show up today. I'm so excited." She races into the room, stopping long enough to hug Katie.

"Katie, won't you introduce us to your little friend?" Mom asks.

"Mom, Dad, this is Nurse Sonya. Nurse Sonya this is my mom and dad, Brenda Mae and Bobby Joe."

"Hello Brenda Mae and Bobby Joe," Nurse Sonya states.

"Honey, I've been trying to call your brother all day," Mom picks up the receiver. "I just know something bad has happened to him. Please tell me everything is all right. Please."

Katie glances toward Sonya and motions her to the doorway. "I'll be right back and we can talk about Stan in a minute." Katie and Sonya move toward the door. "What the hell is she talking about? She hasn't asked about Stan in over a year. She hasn't recognized me in two. I don't get it."

"Do you want to tell her Stan is dead?" Sonya asks.

Katie sighs and gazes back over at her parents. She thought she had made a difficult decision when she put them in the home, but telling them about Stan, that might be even worse.

CHAPTER TWENTY-SEVEN

Maddy stares out the window and shivers. Split wood is stacked up against a large shed. She wonders for the hundredth time how she might be able to carry several loads up the stairs with the twenty pound ball hanging off her left ankle. *Thank God they finally unhooked the chains from the bed but this isn't helping me to get the wood here. Where is Mickey and Candy Sue? It feels like years since I last saw them.*

Stepping over to the small crib, Maddy pulls the covers up over the baby. She turns her attention to the small wooden stove in the corner. Only a few small blocks of wood are left in the wood box by the stove. It won't be long before she has to start breaking up furniture. "It's going to be okay." She slides two more small blocks onto the embers and watches as the flames engulf them and radiates a layer of heat.

Rubbing her hands together, she picks up the poker and moves the ashes and wood around. "Okay, now let's see what food I have left." Ambling over to the small kitchen area, Maddy opens several cabinet doors. Food is plentiful. "We just need to get wood."

Maddy makes her way toward the bathroom. Taking her seat on the throne, her eyes search for the spot in the corner she remembers seeing from a week earlier. A loose floorboard. She hadn't noticed it when she first came here. She hadn't had a chance to investigate because for most days someone was always nearby until almost a week ago.

"I gotta go away for a couple of days," Candy Sue says, as she brings in another load of wood. She and Maddy had stacked the wood neatly close to the wooden stove. There had been at least four ricks.

"Where are you going?" Maddy had asked. *I kept asking and she kept saying she had work. I asked about the her ball and chain.* "I gotta get us some wood," was Candy Sue's only answer.

Maddy picks at the edge of the wood and tries not to mar it, making sure to keep all the pieces perfectly intact. "Will have to make this right when I'm done exploring."

The small rectangle pops out easily. Five more follow with ease.

Plunging her hand into the small space, Maddy gasps when she feels the web covered journal. Even with the dirt, she sees the pink. She gently eases it out of

218

the small opening. Dusting it off, she turns to the first page and nearly falls off the toilet.

> To whoever may read this: my name is Shoshana Meyers and I need your help.

Shoshana Meyers, isn't she the horror writer who disappeared? Ohmygosh … what the hell happened to her? She escaped. She's the reason I'm wearing a chain with a ball the size of … attached to my leg. Maddy listens intently but all she hears is silence. She places the book on her knees and quickly reassembles the hiding spot.

What happened to you, Shoshana? How did you escape? She makes her way back into the makeshift bedroom/kitchen. She strolls around the room, searching for a possible new hiding spot and finally decides to place it between the mattresses for now.

She grabs a bottle of water from the kitchen and makes her way toward the rocking chair in front of the window. Opening the bottle, she takes a quick sip before putting the lid back on and setting it on the ledge.

She opens the book and stares at the first page.

It isn't bad here but I really want to go home. Mickey and Candy Sue are a little strange but okay. I just like home better. I haven't seen Mickey or Candy Sue in days. Mickey wasn't looking too good the last time I saw him. Candy Sue says he sometimes gets pretty depressed. Disappears for a little while. Where is he? Where is Candy Sue? I have to do something.

Maddy thumbs through the rest of the book and it takes her a moment for her to realize that the first page is actually the last. The pages are full of words and pictures describing things Shoshana had seen while she was captive here. Sighing loudly, Maddy swipes the tears racing down her cheeks. *I'm never going to leave this place, am I?*

At first she didn't have a problem being here. It was as good a place as any to be. She had a home with food, water, love and then things started to change. When she asked for a book to read to break the monotony of the silence she was slapped so hard she thought her eye would pop out of its socket.

Picking up the chain, she stares down at the lock.

+++

Picking up the journal, I flip through the pages once more. It's a move I've made many times since coming upon it. Each time I see it something new pops out to me. I know it has the makings of a really great book, if I chose to go that path.

I have no doubt that it would make a great novel, if not a best seller.

"You have to give it to the detectives, you know that, don't you?" Deborah asks, as she enters the office.

I nod. "Yeah, I know, but how? This was a big part of my life." I giggle as I flip to a page with a picture. "Can you see them trying to get guys to line up that look like this?" I point to the Herman Munster/Frankenstein monster drawing. The creature is tall with large shoulders and large hands. Several large scars race across the man's cheeks and broken nose. His forehead is high and long hair dangles past his waist.

Deborah sniggers and shakes her head. "I can see it now. Calling all cars, calling all cars ... we have a Fred Gwynn lookalike on the move."

We both crack up laughing. "We're old, girlfriend. I don't think too many people know who Fred Gwynn is these days."

"Can you imagine when they call me to a line up? If it was Halloween, they would have all sorts of crazies in there. Okay, miss, which twelve-year-old do you think did it?" I giggle.

222

Shaking her head, she pats my shoulder. "You're so silly. Haven't you found anything that might help?"

Flipping the book over, I show her the first page. "Apparently this wasn't the first of these. There's another one with the details of the captivity." I sigh. "I was kept somewhere, somewhere with mountains because I have lots of pictures of mountains and the creatures there. So the question is … how did I get from that place in the mountains to a Harlem alley?"

+++

Mr. George glances at the caller ID before answering his cell. "Yes."

"We need to have a meet and greet, old friend," the male voice states.

Mr. George swallows loudly. Sweat beads form on his upper lip and forehead, dripping down into his shirt collar. His palms dampen and already there are stains on the inside of his clean white dress shirt armpits. *Damn deodorant. What the hell good is it if it can't even take eighty degree heat? This ain't the heat, is it? It's mixing life and death, and not coming out on top.* He sighs. "Yes sir."

"The driver will pick you up in five. This is a meeting you don't want to miss." Click.

Grabbing up the bottle of scotch from the bar, he unscrews the lid and tosses it on the floor. He chugs its contents. It burns the back of his throat as well as the inside of his stomach. Tears slide onto his already damp shirt. He keeps drinking. When he finally stops, the almost full bottle is empty. He lets it slide to the marble floor and watches as it shatters, sending glass splinters everywhere … a metaphor for his life at this moment, and he knows it.

Gasping and coughing, he sputters and moans. Despite all the alcohol, he feels sober. Too sober. But there's no time to stop that now. He makes his way to the lobby.

Just as he reaches the lobby, he spots the black stretch limo pulling up.

The driver helps him from the doorman to the door and inside.

Mr. George slumps down into the seat. He can barely see the world around him as he lies on the plush leather.

"This will never work," a voice whispers in the distance, as he grabs Mr. George's arm. He rolls up the other man's sleeve and applies a tourniquet.

"Please, let me die," Mr. George slurs, as the other person searches for a vein."I have money. I can pay you. All you have to say is I had a heart attack on the way. You didn't want to risk taking me to the hospital so … "

The young man hits the vein, and grins as he releases the tourniquet.

Mr. George can do nothing as the drug surges through his alcohol coated blood to his heart. It skips a beat before taking off at a hundred miles an hour. The nausea is slight, just enough to let him know he is alive. The pressure in his brain pulsates in his eyes and ears. *Oh my God, I don't have to worry. I really am going to have a heart attack and die. Thank God.*

"It's not time to die," the young man whispers, as he tugs on Mr. George's pants. Sliding them to his knees, the young man reaches for Mr. George's penis.

Mr. George flinches and tries to pull away but his body refuses his command. *This isn't about sex, is it? This is about suffering, but he wanted me to teach them all lessons. So why is he punishing me?* Mr. George gasps as his eyes clear and he takes in the back of the limo.

A mattress lies in the middle of the floor. Shackles are attached to the corners.

"It's a shame. You have such nice equipment too." The young man's soft caress brings Mr. George's large penis to a fuller than full erection.

Mr. George moans softly and lets his eyes roll back in his head.

"I bet you'd pay pretty good right now for me to suck you off."

Mr. George gazes up at the young blond's full lips and wide grin. "Oh God, yes. What is your name?"

"You can call me Alisha," the young man answers.

"Alisha? Alisha, why don't you come over and do what I want?" Mr. George asks, as he stares into the young man's deep blue eyes.

"You mean like this?" Alisha drops to his knees and smirks at the older man. His lips meet Mr. George's and his tongue pushes toward Mr. George's waiting ones.

God, I want him. I want him now. Where the hell is Mr. Big? Why aren't we meeting with him right now? Not that I mind the delay but really, really, should I be worrying? Oh, God, I'm so fucking horny I could scream.

"Having fun I see." A familiar voice states.

Gasping and pulling away from Alisha, Mr. George glances around the room before catching sight of the flat screen popping up from the wet bar.

Mr. Big's smiling face beams back at him. His perfect dark hair makes you think he may have made a deal with the devil to keep his looks so youthful.

"I, uh," Mr. George's face burns against the collar of his shirt and jacket. His heart races in his chest, as he reaches down to cover up his erection with the tail of his tailored shirt. It doesn't do any good. He doesn't remember a time when he was this erect. Always enough to play and have a good time but not like this, this is even bigger than when he was a teenager.

"You said men couldn't get you so hot, didn't you?" Mr. Big voices with a light chuckle.

"What the hell did your man give me?" Mr. George whines.

Snickering loudly, Mr. Big shakes his head. "Nothing you haven't had before."

"I thought we were meeting face to face." Mr. George grasps the soft seat and squeezes with all his might. *Oh God, I really need to fuck something. It hurts. I just need to cum.*

"Our last face to face was our last face to face," Mr. Big answers. "It has come to my attention that many of the pieces are dropping and those pieces are trying to make their way back to me."

Mr. George's eyes widen. He knows questioning Mr. Big is out of the question but his mouth moves despite his desire to keep silent. "Is that why we killed

Mary Elizabeth? Stan? I thought they were great ponsies. What about that Shoshana bitch? Aren't we going to take care of her too?" The thought of her wrapping her lips around his organ makes him shudder.

"You guys already clusterfucked that one to death," Mr. Big answers, as he puffs on his cigar.

Mr. George gasps and moans. *This is when I should be losing my erection. So my death is next. Oh God, what are they going to do to me? Oh God, please be merciful to me. I'm so sorry I hurt them. I couldn't help myself.*

"What was our one rule?" Mr. Big asks.

"We could do whatever we wanted as long as we kept the women coming and the drugs flowing." Mr. George sighs.

"What is the rest of that rule?"

"Never to touch your family, or anyone we were told was off

limits." *Oh God, oh God. Alisha?*
Alisha. Oh God, Alisha. New tears
form in the corners of his eyes
as a picture flashes on the
screen and in his mind. A young
woman by the name of Alisha. Her
was hair the color of cotton
balls. His eyes shut as his mind
drifts back in time. He stares at
the television screen as moaning
echoes from it.

CHAPTER TWENTY-EIGHT

Mr. George's eyes widen as
the young woman's face appears
before the camera.

"You have such a lovely
place." She giggles and pushes
her breasts up and almost out of
her low cut blouse.

"Thank you." Mr. George
grins and hands her a drink.

She turns around and plants
a large kiss on his face before
taking the drink and downing it.
"I love the earrings." She puts

the glass down on the small table beside them, and cups her earlobes, showing off the two carat ice decorations. "They're so gorgeous. Oh baby, you're the most generous man I've ever met. It makes me want to suck you long time."

She drops to her knees and pulls his robe aside. Her lips wrap around his manhood.

He shudders and grasps the small table with one hand, while wrapping his other hand around that sensuous blondeness. "That's it, bitch. Make me happy. "

Mr. George's hands tremble as they wrap around his penis and give a good yank. His eyes search the screen for whatever he's missing. *Yeah, I liked her. She was good for about ten seconds.*

"You got careless, didn't you?"

A new picture slides across the screen. The face is gone and only a hollowness takes its place. "Oh my God!" Mr. George gasps.

"You made a deal with her, didn't you? You paid her to act like she was in love with Stan? Wasn't that the plan? She was to seduce him and get to the millions of that fucking horror writer's monies, but what went wrong?"

Mr. George shakes his head. "I don't know," he whispers.

"She fell in love with that schmuck. She paid a couple to get them to pretend they were her sister and brother-in-law just so she could see if he was in love with her. All along she was in love with you. She was a fucking virgin when she met you, and you turned her into a whore," the voice rasps louder.

"I, uh. I don't know what to say."

Mr. Big sighs. "I always try to keep business and family separate. Something I felt the mafia would have been better off if they had, but then the whole loyalty thing … " he sighs. "You have to fear from those who would sell their own mothers for thirty pieces of silver."

"I don't understand," Mr. George states.

Alisha leans over and grasps Mr. George's penis.

"Alisha or Honey, as Stan knew here, was my daughter. If you had gone to the people above you before you picked her, you would have known that. You met her at one of my functions. How stupid were you to think you could use and abuse and … " Tears roll down the big man's face, he does nothing to stop or conceal them. "You did the most unthinkable things to my daughter and now you must pay."

Mr. George gasps as Alisha applies a tourniquet to his erection.

Tightening it, Alisha grins and whispers. "Baby, you won't be needing this anymore. Your cute little pussy is going to feel so good and tight against my big ass dick. Honey," he shakes his head.

"open your mouth for the big surprise."

Mr. George's screams echo off the sides of the limo, as he stares out the windows and realizes they are now parked in an empty warehouse.

+++

"You're a little nervous giving this to me, aren't you?" Olivia asks, as she takes the journal from my outstretched hands.

I nod. "It could get into the wrong hands."

She sighs. "I tell you what. I will leave it here, and will only take pictures of what I think is necessary. That way the book will still be with you the rest of the time."

"I have a copy machine. I have no problem with making copies."

"Are you remembering anything more? Have you even been to the alley?" Olivia asks.

"What good would that do?" Deborah asks. "It's obvious Stan was in on all of this. Maybe he did it all and now he's dead. What good would it be to make a fuss now?"

Olivia nods toward Kevin. "We think there's more to it. That's why we posted someone downstairs. We really feel like your lives are in danger."

Deborah gasps and races toward me. Wrapping her arms around me, she pulls me closer.

"What about Deborah's family? If this is some sort of revenge, wouldn't they be in danger too?" I ask.

Olivia and Kevin nod toward each other once more.

"We need to check on that a little more. All we know is that we now have four dead bodies."

I shiver and stare into the woman's eyes. Her partner turns away and I know they're both hiding something.

"When did you lose your identity?" Olivia whispers.

"Probably before I started writing in this book. Oh God, what made me so scared that I blocked out my whole life?"

+++

Securing the fire, Maddy looks in on the baby. She picks up the bucket before leaning down and grasping the twenty pound metal ball in both hands. She leaves just enough chain to keep from tripping over it, and slowly makes her way toward the door. She suddenly realizes she hasn't left this room in months.

Slowly, she turns the handle and pushes. She half expects Candy Sue or Mickey to leap out and shove her back inside, but there is only emptiness. She shuffles across the wooden floor. The ball isn't heavy just awkward.

Maddy stumbles into the long hallway and glances around. The stairs are a million miles away and yet they are really only fifty feet from her. She tries not to trip over the chain, as she makes her way toward them. *You can do it. You can do it.* Her mind races faster than her bare feet on the stairs. She expects them to creak and is surprised when they don't.

When she reaches the bottom, she gazes around the living room/dining room combo and gasps. It's perfect. All of the furniture is older but clean. For a minute, she believes she's in a doll house. *Gotta hurry. There's a baby waiting for me.* She sighs.

The next ten steps feel like a dream as her body moves toward the door and freedom. Juggling the ball in one hand, she reaches for the door handle with the other. Seconds later, she steps out into the bright sunshine and lifts her face toward the bright rays. She smiles. A chill is in the air but it's nothing compared to the heat from the sunshine.

Inhaling deeply, Maddy lets the oxygen fill her lungs. Raising her hands above her head, Maddy opens her hands wide. She gasps as she looks down in time to see the metal ball miss her big toe by two inches. It hits the ground with a dull thud. Her heart skips a beat before it races out of control. "Oh God, I'm such an idiot."

She gazes over at the wood pile. She grabs for the pail with one hand and the ball with the other. Balancing them both, she makes her way across the snow covered walkway. She stares at her surroundings and sighs. From her window, Maddy can only see the wood shed and chopping block as well as part of a garage.

First things first, she eases the ball to the ground and fills the bucket with wood. "Hello!" she calls out.

Silence.

"Hello."

Nothing.

Maddy shrugs and continues to fill the bucket. When it's full, she picks it up, as well as the ball and starts back. Her heart pounds in her chest, and she realizes it isn't from fear. "I'm really getting out of shape but then I don't remember carrying a ball like this before." She giggles. *I think the next order of the day is to try to figure out how to get this damn ball off.*

+++

"Dare we check out that alley again?" Kevin asks, as they head back to the car.

Olivia snickers. "I don't know. Every time we do we find another body. It's like these things are just falling from the sky. Maybe the alley is a time portal."

"You caught yourself, didn't you?"

Olivia glares at him.

"You were going to say of the sick and depraved, weren't you?"

Olivia sighs. "Well, we do seem to be finding a lot of weird things in that alley."

"The city might want to put surveillance cameras there but then in that location it would never last. They'd either break it or rip it off for money or parts." Kevin's cell rings and he catches it on the second ring. "Yeah."

Silence.

"What's that address? We're right on it." He shuts the phone and slides it into his pocket. "Speaking of the devil, guess where we need to go?"

"Hell Alley?"

Kevin nods as they get into the car.

Thirty minutes later, they pull up to the familiar yellow tape, and black and whites.

Olivia leaps from the car before Kevin even has it in park. She dashes around the corner just in time to come face to face with a female uniformed officer. She recognizes her from Stan's apartment.

She shakes her head. "This is another prize." She sighs before making her way to the sidewalk and vomiting.

Olivia inhales deeply, letting the air flow through her lungs, and giving life to her brain. *It's going to be okay. Just keep puppies and kitties in your mind. You can do it.* She sighs. "Okay." She spots the body seconds later.

"I'm pretty sure this one is a message," Kevin voices from behind her.

"How's that?" Olivia stands over the naked male body.

Something large protrudes from the man's mouth. His eyelids are open and the eyes are dull. Carved in his chest are the words "die, bitch, die". His fingers are missing as well. Where his penis was is nothing but a huge whole.

CHAPTER TWENTY-NINE

Olivia stares at the picture in the plastic evidence bag. *Where have I seen this picture before?*

"Are you still looking at that damned thing?" Kevin picks up his cell, and stares at the text message before turning his attention back to her.

"Yes, you know it's not every day we see a dead man with his penis sticking out of his mouth. Oh my God, I know where I saw this picture." Shifting several folders around, Olivia picks up Shoshana's and flips it open. "Shoshana made copies of about ten pages for me. This," she holds up the baggie covered photo, "is the same as this one." She picks up the folder and lines it up with the other picture.

He gasps. "Holy shit."

A large man adorns the paper. His long hair is tangled and sticking out all over his head like he has had his hand in the electric socket way too long. Many of his teeth are missing, and two large scars cover both cheeks coming to a point on his forehead. His misshapen nose adds to the gruesomeness.

"Again, add green and he would be looking like Herman Munster," Kevin adds.

Olivia rolls her eyes. "Enough with the funnies. He's our killer."

Kevin sighs and shakes his head. "I don't think so."

"What makes you think it isn't him?" Olivia asks. She stares down at both papers. On the photocopy two words caption it: **Mountain Man.**

"I think we need to go see Carolyn," Kevin says.

"I think you are right." Olivia grabs up her cell before

they make their way to the stairs.

+++

Katie steps into Stan's old bedroom and frowns. When she had moved out, Mom and Dad had made a sewing room for Mom into her room, but Stan's room was just as he had left it. The only change is a large scrapbook in the middle of the bed, and an even larger picture of Stan in his hay day hung up on the back of the closet door.

Every where she looks there are mirrors, all dust covered and cobwebby. She takes a seat on the bed and picks up the scrapbook. She glances through the pages stopping when she arrives at Stan's wedding announcement. He looks so handsome and Shoshana is gorgeous.

"She was so much better than you," Katie says, as she flips to the next page. A picture slips from the last five unused pages. It slides to the floor, face down.

She picks it up. On the backside it says: mountain cabin home. On the front there is a picture of a two story cabin. A small blue garage shed sits kitty corner to it. The house looks almost foreign with the blue coloring. It almost looks as if someone got bored and got spray cans of different blue paints and just started spraying the wood. She can't imagine Stan calling something as primitive as it home. Her parents' home is better and he always told them it was a slum that he couldn't wait to leave.

+++

"So, are you sure these cases are all related?" Olivia asks, as she and Kevin take seats in front of Carolyn's desk.

Carolyn nods and reaches for her cup of coffee on the other side of the desk.

Kevin grabs it and hands it to her.

"Thank you. Yes, I am." Carolyn gives Olivia the other

two files with the recent reports on Stan, Mary Elizabeth and their recent find. It's of two Jane Does.

Olivia glances through them both and grins. "They both had the same drugs in their systems. They both had the same wounds."

"They were both brutalized in the same manner, as well as the bite marks," Carolyn states.

Olivia flips to the pictures in one, and hands it to Kevin before finding the pictures in the second file. "At least their faces are still intact even if their teeth and fingers were missing."

Carolyn takes another sip of coffee. "I'm glad they left their faces on. I also found DNA on one of the girls and guess who it matches?"

"Stan?" Kevin asks.

Olivia smirks. "The guy from yesterday?"

"Bingo! We have a winner. Those two aren't the only bodies that have showed up all over town. I've contacted some of the other coroners in the five boroughs, and they all confirm they have found female bodies with the same MO. Some have been a little more mutilated than others, but most are between fifteen and twenty-five. All have been raped and tortured."

"Do they have DNA on all of them?" Kevin asks.

"No, most of them don't, but then most of them were found either in the water or close by water. I want to show you something else about your man from yesterday." Carolyn stands and makes her way back over to the two slabs.

Olivia and Kevin are right on her heels.

"What did you find that was unusual other than a man with a penis in his mouth?" Olivia asks.

Kevin shudders. "Do you have to keep saying that?"

248

"If you can keep talking about looking for a Fred Gwynn look-a-like, then I can keep saying man with a penis in his mouth."

Carolyn chuckles.

Kevin shudders.

"How do you two get anything done is beyond me." She stops at the first body and pulls down the sheet. The man's eyes are still open.

"What's with his eyelids?" Olivia asks.

"Well, this is a new one. I have to admit I have seen it before but only in extreme organized crime cases. That's very rare. Someone burnt his eyes with a cigar."

Olivia and Kevin gasp as they stare down at the burnt out hollows of his eye sockets.

"At first I thought there was garbage and such in his eyes but then as I started to inspect them, well, they looked better

before I had to dissect them."
She sighs. "The worst part is … "

"What could be worse?" Kevin
asks.

"He must have really pissed
someone off because this was done
while he was still alive."

+++

Yawning, I reach over and
grab for another blanket. I
snuggle it a little closer to my
breast. It isn't really cold, but
I feel a little chilly. "Well, I
wonder if I should be working on
a zombie book or a ghost book
today." It's always exciting when
I get to start a new book.

"What the fuck you mean,
start a new book?" a low,
southern drawl asks.

"Huh?"

"You know you don't know how
to read and write, you dumb
fucking slut. Shut your trap and
go get me something to eat."

I gasp as I look over at the other side of the bed and see it's empty. "What the heck?" My heart skips a beat and I leap to my feet, and almost stumble on the baby's bassinet. "Oh my gosh, what the heck just happened?"

Glancing down at Chanah, I pull the blanket back up over her big shoulders.

She's growing. She's so much bigger than I was when I was her age.

Now all I need to do is get that book. I know who that creature is in that picture. He ain't the handsomest man in the world, but we did do something didn't we? We created a baby together. I turn on the baby monitor and grab the handheld one to take with me. I'm thankful that Deborah is now sleeping in the bedroom on the other side of the apartment. I love my sister dearly, but she can be a little bossier than I like, but then she has been a mother longer than I have.

Flipping on the desk light, I take my seat. The book is right next to the keyboard. I inhale deeply, and let the oxygen fill me up. "I shouldn't be so afraid. It's just a book." *A book that holds the key to all the mysteries of the past year or so. My mysteries.* I flip through the pages to the same one that I had made a copy of for Olivia and Kevin.

Staring at the clock, I frown. It's only five A.M. It's too early to call the detectives. There's only one thing I can do, write. I click the computer on, I can always catch a nap when the baby does later on.

CHAPTER THIRTY

Katie stares down at the deed. *When did Mom and Dad purchase this one?* She picks up the scrapbook. "So, brother, I'm guessing this is another part of the secret life you kept from us. Why? Oh why did you have to turn out this way? Why would you want an ugly blue cabin?"

+++

Deborah races to the kitchen after Olivia and Kevin takes their usual seats.

"This is getting to be a regular date," I giggle.

"Well, your sister does make a mean cup of Joe," Kevin answers.

"But seriously, what do you think you have found?" Olivia asks.

"The picture I gave you," I stare down at Chanah as she plays with her rattle.

She jabbers away, all the while drooling and grinning.

"It's a picture of her father," it comes out so soft that I can bearly hear it myself. I have no clue if they have heard it until I stare up into Olivia's eyes.

"Are you remembering more?" Olivia asks, as she jumps to her feet.

I lean forward and grasp the journal lying on the coffee table. Flipping the pages, I spot one of the entries. It's a poem. "You already have the picture so I don't have to give that to you. Have you ever heard of Beverly, West Virginia?"

+++

Mr. Big picks up his phone. "Bring her in."

The tall dark haired man steps into the room, pulling a tall woman with him.

She struggles against his rough hands. Thick ropes tighten about her wrists and ankles. They bite into the tender white skin with each step. She whimpers softly over the bandana gag dangling from her mouth. "Please help me," she mumbles over it. Tears streak down her cheeks.

The dark haired man shoves the woman on the floor, and kicks her backside forward.

She flops down on the thick carpet face first. Coughing and sputtering, she kicks out until she manages to flip over.

"I have a good mind to piss on her," the brunette hisses.

Mr. Big chuckles, and steps around his desk. "I told you not to hurt her. If she is harmed in any way, I will personally cut off your balls." He eyes the brunette.

The younger man cowers, edging his way toward the door.

"Don't fucking run away from me, you little coward. Take the damn gag out of her mouth. I don't want her to choke to death before I'm done with her."

The brunette pulls the woman up on her knees and rips the bandanna away.

"Help!" she screams. "Oh God, please help me."

"Thank you, you may go now."

"Yes, sir." The brunette turns on his heels and races out the door, making sure to lock it behind him.

"Oh, sweetheart, are you all right?" Mr. Big grabs her shoulders and lifts her to a standing position. His hands drift down to her large breasts. He squeezes them.

Tears roll down her cheeks, and she pulls back and almost stumbles over a bump in the carpet. "Aren't you going to help me?"

"Why? Should I?"

She shivers against his ice cold touch.

"Are you Amanda George? Sister of Ted George the successful New York City businessman?" His hands slide over her hips, yanking the tight skirt over them, and letting it fall to the floor.

"What?"

He squeezes her left butt cheek until she screams. "What the fuck is your name, cunt?"

Fresh tears drop from her closed eyes, she shakes her head. She tugs on the ropes and watches as blood drips from the bites on her wrists from them.

"Answer the question."

"Y-y-y-e-e-e-s-s-s-s-s."

"You're prettier than I thought you would be." Mr. Big releases the tight flesh and reached for the underwear band. Ripping it from her flesh, he lets it fall next to the skirt.

"Please don't hurt me," she begs.

"Do you have any idea what your brother did to my daughter, my baby girl?"

She gulps and shakes her head. Her eyes never leave a spot on the carpet. Her trembling body shakes against his icy hands. "My brother?"

"He thought she was a toy. He did the most horrible things to her. Did you know he was a sick pervert that liked to rape and murder young innocent women for his own sexual pleasure?"

"Not my brother."

"Ted George? Ted George with political asperations?"

She hangs her head. "I'm sorry."

Balling up his fist, he punches her in the nose.

Flying backward, she lands flat on her back. She screams as blood spurts from her nose and mouth. She struggles to get back on her feet.

Mr. Big never moves.

"Please, I'm sure he just didn't know she was your daughter."

He shakes his head. Pulling a tazer from his pocket, he presses it against her neck and pulls the trigger.

Her screams echo off the walls as she falls to the ground, her body flopping about the carpet like a fish out of water seconds before the smell of fresh urine fills the air.

Mr. Big slams his foot into her ribcage. "Fucking bitch, we'll never get that smell out of here."

+++

"We have to go to the alley," I whisper to Olivia and Kevin. The words tumble out so quickly I'm sure they didn't hear it.

Deborah is in the bathroom, and I know if she were in the room she would be protesting. It's bad enough that she will have to be with me when I go, but to have her hear it now when I'm unsure … I couldn't do that even to me.

"Are you sure?" Olivia asks.

"It has been what over a month?" I ask.

"Almost two," Kevin answers.

I nod. Time has always been irrelevant to me. That hasn't changed since getting back. "I need to see where my baby was born."

"We might have to get special permission," Kevin states.

Olivia glares in his direction.

"Why?"

"It seems to be a dumping ground of sorts lately," Olivia sighs and answers.

I nod. "Bodies?" *Even before the word leaves my mouth I realize how crazy it sounds. Of course there are bodies. What else would cause such a commotion? I guess one of these days I'm going to have to watch the news or read a paper, but it isn't today.*

"Are you all right?" Deborah asks, as she steps into the room.

She races toward me and feels my forehead.

"I'm okay." I giggle.

"She just thinks she can do anything. The doctor says she still needs to take it easy. I guess when you have a baby her age your body doesn't bounce back as quickly as any other time." Deborah picks up the coffee carafe and refills their cups.

"Sister, I just told them I need to go to the alley where Chanah was born." I sigh and wait for the scream, but there isn't one.

Deborah pours another cup of coffee. Dropping three lumps of sugar in it, she pours a little fresh cream in it before stirring it. She takes a long pull from it before making her way to her seat on the couch.

The silence is almost deadly. For a second it feels like we've all been holding our breaths.

"I think that is an excellent idea." She takes another sip from her cup before balancing it on the arm of the couch and smiling back at us.

"Are you sure?" I ask.

She nods. "I've watched you suffer for a while. You sleep because your body is tired, but you don't always rest well. Sometimes you scream in the night. Sometimes you sit at your desk and scream. I guess you doze for a few seconds. You're restless. You won't go anywhere. You've changed, but of course you've changed. How could you not change after all the things you've been through?"

"I know, that's why I agreed to it. I think there is some sort of clue there that they haven't found."

"About the kidnapping?" Deborah faces Olivia.

"It's more than that."

"How much more?" Deborah asks.

Kevin sighs. "There have been a few more bodies discovered in that alley."

"That's where your manager was found. We don't know how they are all connected other than you, but we are going to keep working on it until we find out."

"I don't think the man is here. I think he is far away in Beverly, West Virginia."

CHAPTER THIRTY-ONE

Even before the car comes to a complete stop, I unbuckle the seatbelt and leap from the car. I crawl under the familiar yellow tape, and dash toward the back of the alley. It isn't really an alley as much as a deep rivulet of trash. An eight foot wooden fence separates it from the rest of the alleyway.

Trash and old clothes line the brick walls and make a carpet on the ground.

How in the world did the ambulance ever get a gurney in here is beyond me. I stare at the colors. They're so bright and alive in such a dark and horrifying place.

Dropping to my knees, I let my hands push through the eight inch deep clothing and pull something from it. It's a small blood covered satchel. I hold it up as the tears drip down my burning cheeks. A shiver races up and down my spine as my heart skips a beat. The blood pulsates in my head so hard I know it will explode but it doesn't. These aren't tears of fear and pain, but tears of survival and insight.

+++

Maddy opens up the small sewing kit. Gazing out the window, she checks for any signs of life. Nothing. She stares at Baby Girl playing with the makeshift rattle of skeleton keys she found around the room. "Momma just needs to get this damn ball off her ankle, and we can try to figure out how to get out of here."

The baby coos and smiles. Drool drips down her chin onto her soft pink shirt, she scrunches up her eyebrows and bites the metal.

The lock is small and not very complicated. Despite looking in every possible hiding spot, Maddy's clueless for the key. She thrusts the small needle into the lock and listens for the familiar clicks of contact. Nothing. She sighs loudly before changing needles. Picking up the larger needle, she flips it around to the eye end.

Slipping it back into the lock, she strains her ears for the sounds. Clicks, any clicks would be music to her ears. She stops and listens for familiar sounds of stairs and humans.

Baby Girl giggles.

"That's a good girl. I think mama has it this time." Maddy smiles at her baby. Her hands tremble as the first click vibrates the lock. She tightens her grip on the lock and needle and goes for click number two. *What did Shoshana say? Oh yeah, that if Candy Sue and Ole Mickey disappear for more than two weeks it's time to escape. Something about how they both struggle with depression but that if they disappear it might be because they are dead.*

Seconds later, the lock pops open. Tears flow from her eyes, Maddy loosens the four inch wide fetter from her ankle. She snaps it back together and slides the lock back into place, clicking it closed. Grasping her ankle, she rubs the raw yet calloused skin. She stretches her foot, flexing the ankle and every muscle and bone.

"Oh my God, Oh my God," she whispers. She swipes at the tears, but they flow down her face and onto her top. Her eyes widen as she leaps and dances around the room.

Baby Girl giggles.

+++

"How thorough have your people been here?" I stare around the alley. Everything looks strange and yet very familiar to me. I reach back and tighten the baby sling about my neck. There's no way I'm going to let the garbage reach my baby. Ever again.

"Well, with all the bodies we keep finding here, I'd say it's been getting a regular shake down," Kevin answers.

"Ever find anything other than bodies and me?" I ask. I know the answer even before Olivia shakes her head.

"Sweetie, are you sure you don't want me to take the baby?" Deborah asks, at the edge of the entry way.

"No, but I do wish you would either come closer or wait with an officer. I feel like this is a black hole. Your either in it or not." I know my sister well enough to know she's not going to risk ruining a pair of Manolos even for me.

"Please don't ask me to do that," Deborah begs.

Eying Olivia, I motion toward my sister.

"I got this one." Olivia makes her way back to Deborah.

"What are you looking for?" Kevin asks, as several police cars pull up.

"I don't know yet. I feel like I know this place well. Like maybe it was my part time house." Dropping to my knees, I reach under the mattress until my hand hits something hard. I grasp it and pull it out. It's a small metal box. I open it and gasp. A cell phone and a wad of money sit atop another journal.

I pick it up and carry it toward the wall behind the mattress. Reaching under the top, I pull out a small handgun as well as a backpack. I grin at Kevin. "Seems my alter ego is a little more paranoid than I am on a good day."

"Where the hell did that come from?" Kevin backs up as his hand slides to his service revolver at his hip.

"What did you find?" Deborah calls out.

I wink at Kevin. "Seriously, Detective, if I had wanted to kill you or any of you, wouldn't I have done that at my home? These are mine. That I'm sure of." I sniff the air. Probably not something one wants to do in a puke, vomit and shit infested alley, but something I need to do.

All three invade my nostrils, and I gasp to choke back the bile in the back of my throat begging to escape. Thank God I ate some toast before coming here. I inhale deeply, letting the stale air fill my lungs.

"Sorry, it's just reflex. You know we will have to check the gun out."

I nod. I have nothing to hide. I hand the gun to Kevin.

269

How many times have I slept in this alley? Where else could I go? I guess going underground in Grand Central Station wasn't safe enough for me. I sigh. Standing up, I make my way toward the left hand corner closest to the wooden fence.

Bending over, I shove several layers of trash off the high pile. Beneath it is another layer, I toss it aside as well to reveal a small pup tent. My pup tent.

"Oh my God, you were living in this frigging alley?" Deborah gasps.

"Home sweet home," I whisper, as I unzip it and glance inside. "No bodies here," I snicker.

"How the hell did you even get in there?" Kevin asks, as he reaches down and pulls it up and out of its small space.

Trash and rotten clothing cling to the bottom despite his shaking the tent to dislodge them. It rattles.

"Be careful," I remind him, "this was my home at one time. There might be clues to what my life was like back then."

He sighs and nods. "Anything else?"

Gazing around the alley way, I listen to my heart beat. It pounds against my breastbone as if it's trying to play out Ricky Ricardo's Babaloo from "I Love Lucy".

Chanah wraps her hand around my coat lapel and tugs on it.

"Hi Sweetie," I coo back. My heart skips a beat as I hear screaming.

+++

"I know I don't normally leave town but I have an emergency," Katie states, as she gives Sonya her spare cell phone.

"I will take the best care of your parents ever," Sonya answers.

Katie nods. "I will. I've left all contacts on the cell. If anything should happen, please call them immediately. I will come as soon as I can."

"Can you tell me where you're going?"

Katie shudders and shakes her head. "The less you know, the better it will be for you."

She grabs the young woman up in a big bear hug. "I read the newspapers. Please be very careful."

"I will," Katie answers, releasing the nurse's large body and stepping backward almost tripping over a small flower patch.

"You know it's like that day was a dream. They recognized you and knew everyone in their family but us caretakers. Now they are back to where they were, they think their only child died twenty years ago. My guess is if something were to happen to you, they would be the first to know." She sighs.

"It will kill them, won't it?" Katie asks.

Sonya nods. "I fear it would but who knows, maybe being dead isn't such a bad thing after the time they have spent in this earthly limbo."

CHAPTER THIRTY-TWO

"I can't believe you let them bring that filthy thing here," Deborah states, as she walks past the pup tent. She shudders.

"How could I not? This was my home for a while and it may give me some sort of clue to how I got here. My guess is that I figured that alley was so scary that no one would even dream of coming in it. Safety thinking even when I don't know who I am, sounds like me."

"How bad was it?" Noah asks. He circles it and grins. "I have to admit I can't imagine you sleeping in that thing. How did you cook?"

I shrug. "I wish I could remember." I smiggle. "My guess is that if I look deep enough in that trash pit I could find a cooker or at least something I used to give off heat."

He nods.

Deborah shudders again. "Did you catch the smell of the tent? She will never get that smell out of this place. This beautiful place and that beast, it's appalling."

I giggle. "That's just the aroma de city. It doesn't smell nearly as bad as it did when I pulled it out. You just aren't used to it."

Deborah frowns. "That's an odor I never want to get used to."

"So what did you find in there?" Noah asks.

Sighing, I eye the small pup tent. "We found that the NYPD

aren't very good at picking through a crime scene. Seriously, we found that even when I live in the outside world, I'm still pretty anal but we also found a few baby things."

Noah snickers.

"Just kidding, I'm sure the NYPD is doing their best." I roll my eyes.

"She found that she can survive anywhere, and that I didn't know my sister as well as I thought I did." Deborah shakes her head and clasps her hands to her hips.

+++

"I'll get this one," Mary, the petite maid voices, as she looks about for her cleaning partner.

"Okay, I'll get the next one." Sandra points toward the next door. She drags her cleaning cart to the door. She picks up a couple of clean towels, and reaches for the doorknob.

"Did you bring your lunch today?" Mary asks.

Sandra nods. "I think we should take a cigarette break after these two rooms. If you finish first, come help me. If I finish, I'll help you, either way we can get this out in less than thirty."

Mary smiles and raps lightly on the door. She checks her chart and frowns. The couple isn't supposed to check out for two more days. She hates trying to clean rooms that still have residents in them. It's much easier when they have already checked out. You get in too much trouble when you clean a room where a resident is still inside.

She shudders and knocks louder. "Maid service!"

Nothing.

Pulling her key from her pocket, she slides it in the slot. It clicks open. She steps inside and glances in the small kitchen. *Well, at least that room is clean. Now for the clean*

sheets and trash and … Walking
into the bedroom, she trips over
the large boot lying in the
middle of the floor.

Her hands fly out in front
of her to catch her from hitting
the corner of the bed and floor.
She grasps something cold and
stiff and stares up at her full
hand. Screams echo against the
sound proof walls, as she stares
at the sized sixteen foot in her
clasp. "Oh my God! Oh my God!"

Dropping the foot, she
screams once more. She glares at
the rest of the body attached to
the foot. Mary's heart skips a
beat as she shakes her hand,
trying to get the feeling of dead
off it. Leaping to her feet, she
races to the doorway almost
falling over the boot again.
"Help! Someone please help me!"

Sandra races out of the
other room as several residents
open their doors and stare out.
It's still fairly early, but with
the new continental breakfast
most people are out of bed by
7:30. Nothing like hot eggs and
sausage to get a body going, and

get people out of their rooms so they can be cleaned.

"Help me," Mary gasps, as tears streak down her pale cheeks. Her eyes widen as she glances over at the startled residents. *Shit, shit, shit … now I'm going to lose this job too. Why can't people die at other fucking hotels? Or the alley? This is fucking nuts.* She reaches into her pocket for a cigarette and remembers the fire alarms.

"It's okay," Sandra states to the others. She watches them make their way back into their rooms, mumbling something about how it's too early for loud noises. "Please go back to your rooms. She probably pulled the shower curtain down or something." Sandra giggles and shrugs before grabbing Mary's shoulder and shoving her back into the room. "What the hell are you thinking? Are you trying to get us into trouble? We have one more strike and we're out. "

"I'm thinking there's a dead body in this fucking room and I need to tell someone." Her hands tremble, as she pushes her friend toward the beds.

"They're probably just sleeping. This room is pretty cold." Sandra shivers and glances up at the air vent blowing cold air. "I don't know why anyone would have the air on when it is freezing outside. There's some strange people in this world."

"Maybe because they wanted to keep the bodies on ice," Mary answers.

"Who would want cold bodies?" Sandra asks, as she makes her way to the man's face. She cringes and shakes her head. "Well, this one ain't gonna win no prizes." She shakes the man's shoulder. "Sir, sir," even before she says it she knows it's useless. She reaches for the man's wrist and frowns. "Yeah, he's dead all right. Check the woman."

Mary gasps and stumbles across the room. Her hands tremble as she reaches for the woman's face. It's ice cold.

Sandra picks up the telephone receiver. "Yeah, this is Gomer in room 813. We got two on ice in here."

Mary fights the bile rising in the back of her throat. "Oh God, I think I'm going to be sick," she mumbles, as she makes her way toward the bathroom.

The stench hits her even before the towels and clothes that are strewn about the floor and over the sink vanity. She grabs her nostrils and pinches them tightly, but it hits her stomach anyway. She leans toward the toilet seat and gasps. Vomit spews across the wall and bathtub, coloring both in blue and red from the fresh blueberries and strawberries Mary had for breakfast.

Blood and bowel contents cover the toilet seat and line the inside of the bowl. A few broken rubbers lie open amongst it.

"Now what?" Sandra runs into the room, glaring at her partner and then over at the toilet. She gazes over to the countertop and grins. Several good sized drug filled condoms sit amongst the used towels. "Jackpot."

"Here," she grabs them up and gingerly judges their weights.

"No," Mary gasps.

"You want a winter coat that will keep you warm and to eat something other than beans?" Sandra whispers.

Staring at the drugs, Mary nods.

"Quick, slip this one in your pantyhose." Sandra slips the slimy rubber into the other woman's hand seconds before taking the other and shoving it down her own.

+++

Olivia and Kevin stare at the full slabs before gazing up at Carolyn.

Both bodies are large. One male and one female.

"Where did these two come from?" Olivia pulls back the sheet from the male victim and grimaces. *He's taller than most and I'm guessing his shoulders are as wide as my hips. Well, almost. Why does this guy look so familiar? Those scars on his face look so familiar. Where have I seen this guy before?* "I still don't understand why we're here."

Carolyn sighs. "I wouldn't normally call you in on a simple drug deal gone wrong but … "

"So, these two were what? Muling and the condoms broke, right?" Kevin asks.

Carolyn nods. "That's what I thought. They were found in an upscale hotel room by the maids. The problem is that when I tested the drugs, I found them to be from the same batch that killed Stan and Honey. You remember, Shoshana Meyers' husband?"

Olivia nods. "And?"

"You know we pretty much get DNA off most people. We got a hit off his DNA."

"And?" Kevin steps closer to the body.

Carolyn clears her throat and stares down at her shuffling feet. She clears it once more before gazing up into Olivia's eyes. "The DNA matches Shoshana's baby's."

Olivia gasps and leans back against the other slab, knocking the dead woman's arm off the table with a loud thud. "What the hell are you talking about?"

"When she gave birth, she let them take a DNA sample in hopes of finding the baby's father. After all we didn't know if the baby was a product of rape or what. The DNA came up with a match all right, twice. The first, parole records, and the second one was when I pulled off a sample from this guy. His finger prints pulled up the name Mickey Dumbinski from West Virginia. The woman is his cousin from the same region."

"Holy shit." Kevin gulps loudly and searches for a chair. "Mind if I sit?" He drops into

283

the office chair and slides across the floor. Grasping the edge of the slab, he makes his way back to his partner and the coroner. His eyes widen as he watches his partner weave and almost fall to the floor.

Grasping Olivia's arms, Carolyn holds up her friend and searches for the other chair. "Hold on. Let's get you in a chair."

"Does she know?" Olivia asks, as she lets her body slide into Kevin's empty chair as he pushes it under her.

"We, my supervisor and I, thought we should talk to you first. This is probably going to be some pretty shocking information for her."

"What else did they find?" Kevin asks.

"I didn't get the full report, but I can tell you this, they'd been traveling either to Canada or from. They had Canadian money and a map of the Niagara Falls area. I'm guessing they

284

were coming from but I could be wrong. Either way … we have two more bodies to your case."

CHAPTER THIRTY-THREE

Olivia reaches for her small backpack and frowns.

"How do you think she's going to take it?" Kevin asks, as he pushes the elevator button.

"I don't know, but if she wasn't making money on her books she could easily become a wealthy artist. Her drawing is uncanny, a deadringer."

Kevin nods.

"Come on in," Deborah says, as she glares at the tent for the hundredth time.

Olivia stifles a giggle.

"Sister … dear sister … that darn thing isn't going to kill you," I snicker.

"It's so ugly. I can't imagine how you can even stand to look at it. It just turns my stomache so." She races off toward the kitchen.

"To be honest, since I brought it here I'm actually sleeping better. Call it crazy, but in a way it's my security blanket." I lead them into the living room. "So what brings you back? Who died now?"

"Well, we don't know how to tell you this," Olivia starts, as she takes her usual seat.

Staring into her eyes, I feel my heart sink to the pit of my stomach. Tears form in my eyes, but they refuse to leave them. "What is it?"

"Do you remember the DNA test they did on the baby?" Kevin asks, pulling lightly on the creases in his well worn black dress pants.

I nod and turn my attention back to Olivia who pulls a small backpack from her back. I don't recall seeing her with a backpack before.

She doesn't carry a purse like most women, but I figure she has big enough pockets in her large coat to supply her needs. "The copy of the picture you gave me as well as the DNA gives us a positive ID of your baby's father and maybe your tormentor."

She pulls a plastic bag out and hands it to me.

My hands tremble as I fumble with the plastic closure. Opening it up, I slide the two pictures onto my lap. "Oh my God!" I place the pictures side by side. My hands fly to my mouth as I stare at the face of the man who kept me captive. "He's the one!"

"What the hell is going on?" Deborah races into the living room nearly dropping the cup laden tray. "What are you doing to my sister?"

Noah steps out from the back bedroom and makes his way toward me.

I gasp for air. My heart and head fill like they are full of helium, and will bounce off of my body if I breathe wrong. My hands grip the papers and I'm thankful they aren't shredding them.

"Shoshana." Deborah wraps her arms around my shoulders and pulls me toward her.

"I remember him. He was with a woman and another man. I remember him. He told me he was going to rape me, and I laughed at him."

"You laughed at him?" Olivia asks.

I shrug. "Why would he rape me? He did two good things for me."

"You mean besides dying?" Kevin asks.

Olivia glares in his direction.

Kevin shrugs.

"What could he possibly do for you?" Deborah asks.

"He gave me the most beautiful daughter in the whole world," I answer, staring over at the pink bassinet.

+++

Maddy takes another bite of the canned meat. It's dry and tasteless in her mouth, but still she eats. She needs her strength. God only knows how long it will take for her to find a town. "I have a carrier for you, and a backpack to carry supplies in." She reaches for the small pouch on the inside of her pants. She managed to find about a hundred dollars stashed away. She hopes that will at least get them some supplies and out of this mess.

+++

Katie stops at the small diner on the outskirts of town. The whole trip so far has been lovely with mountain crests showing through the trees. Even with the light snow, she finds everything beautiful.

The small diner is like all diners. Several tables hold the

morning regulars, and she tries not to listen to their candid banter about life.

"My name is Billie Susan and how may I help you?" Billie Susan the waitress asks.

Katie stifles a giggle as she looks at the woman's beehive of dark red curls. It takes her a second to realize it's a wig. The woman is tall and a little thick around the middle, but from the look of her scuffed shoes, a very hard worker. "A cup of coffee would be a great start. What are your specials?"

"Well, you're in luck, maybe." Billie Susan snickers and eyes the kitchen. "Jimmy Joe is cooking and he likes to make southern delicacies like grits, cornbread and such. We have the southern gentleman breakfast of two eggs over easy, two sausages, grits, hash browns and all the cornbread you can eat."

Katie giggles. "I think I will try that. What's it going to do, kill me?"

Billie Susan chuckles and shakes her head. "With the way he cooks, you just never know."

Seconds later, Billie Susan returns with the coffee pot and fills the small ceramic cup in front of Katie.

Katie grabs up the other cup sitting on the table and turns it over. "Might as well fill this one up too. I'm so thirsty. I don't want to bug you by having you run back and forth to fill my cup."

"Don't worry about it, Miss," one of the large older gentlemen at one of the nearest table voices, "she has plenty of time. It's not like she ever gives me good service." He winks at the waitress as she passes by him.

"You don't pay attention to that old bastard. He gets plenty attention. He just wants everything."

All the regulars break out in laughter.

Katie lowers her shoulders and inhales. *Okay, so the wrong turn people aren't going to kill me today. Maybe this will be a good day after all.*

"So what brings you to Beverly?" Billie Susan asks, as she places a plate full of thick buttered cornbread next to Katie's first cup of coffee.

"Well, I don't know where to begin." She sighs as she lowers her voice. Reaching into her purse, she pulls the picture from it. "My brother died recently. I was looking through his paperwork and I found he had purchased a house close to here. I was wondering if you could tell me where it is, as there wasn't really an address that my GPS understood."

Katie hands Billie Susan the picture.

Taking it, Billie Susan gives a quick glance toward the others.

They're busy trying to blow spit balls at the cook. No one

seems to notice Billie Susan sliding a card over to Katie and slipping it under her coffee cup.

"I don't know if I recognize that one. Could be it's over in the next county and down south." Billie Susan grabs the coffee pot up and refills Katie's cups.

Katie swallows hard and nods. "Thanks, thanks a lot. I knew it was a long shot. I guess I was just a little curious about what my brother was thinking."

"Sorry to hear about your brother. I can tell you this … Beverly is a real nice town to just lose yourself for a day or two. Stay a couple of days and take in the good home cooking and almost winter weather."

"Thank you, I will." Katie gazes around the room again before pulling the card out. The regulars, who are assuredly in their late sixties to early seventies, are still harassing the cook. *Call me at 10 PM. I think I know who you are, and what you need to know.*

+++

"Mr. Big, I think they're ready for you," the tall man in the dark suit steps into the office.

He nods and pushes his chair back from the mahogany desk. "I'll be there in five."

The tall man turns on his heels and steps out, shutting the door behind him.

He stands and strolls toward the mirror. Glancing in the glass, he picks up the small brush and runs it through his thick curly black hair. He grins at himself, revealing the whiter than white teeth the dentist had promised. *Yeah, this is going to be a walk in the park.* He grabs up the Armani suit jacket, and slides his arms into it.

He makes his way toward the crowd waiting for him outside. Nothing like a press conference or a blow job to make one come alive. Either one has people sucking on everything you want to put out there, and still have them begging for more.

"Today, Mr. Mario Bigonzinski would like to give his condolences to the late Mr. Ted George is family," the tall man states into the microphones lined up along a makeshift platform.

Mr. Big steps up and leans toward the microphones. "I just want it to be known that I wish to give my condolences to Mr. George's family. I know what a horrible blow that must be for them. He was on the verge of announcing his resignation from the D. A.s office, and that he was seeking the governor's office. He was a good man," Mr. Big says, as he pulls a handkerchief from his pocket and swipes at the beads of sweat forming on his forehead and upper lip. He presses the starched white cloth to his eyes for effect hoping the sweat will appear as tears in his dry eyes.

"He was a good man," Mr. Big reiterated. *Who loved to rape young girls and watch them get snuffed.* "I know he will be missed. He had a very promising political career. I've spoken to his wife." *Who has no clue how many men this guy has sucked off. God, I'm going to miss his fucking blowjobs. Damn, most women aren't as good as he was.* Tears streak down his cheeks. "I know you all have lots of questions for me and so I'll let Mr. Zander help with the process, I'll try to be as helpful as I can."

CHAPTER THIRTY-FOUR

I step into the morgue with an entourage. I stifle the urge to giggle. We must look hilarious. Me, the baby, Deborah, Noah, Olivia and Kevin all make our way toward the tall woman making her toward us.

"Hey, Olivia and Kevin, is the infamous Shoshana Meyers?" Carolyn asks, as she pulls off her gloves, and puts her hand out to me.

"I don't know about infamous," I giggle, "but that is me."

Her handshake is firm and steady. She shakes hands with Deborah and Noah as well. "My name is Carolyn, and I'm glad to finally meet you. I know you probably hear this a lot, but I've read all your books. I hope you're planning a book about this whole ordeal you've been going through. I think a lot of people would want to read it."

"Thank you, that seems to be the common complaint lately … when are you going to write about your own horror story?" I state, as I glance around the room.

+++

Katie sighs as she rolls over on the bed and glances toward the bedside clock. It's barely 9:30 pm. Her heart skips a beat, as she hears a knock on the door. It's all she can do to keep from running into the bathroom and hiding. "What in the world am I watching on television?" She glances at the screen in time to see the guys see the tattoo on the girl's cooked leg.

Picking up the remote, she flips the television off.

Another knock echoes in the noiseless room.

Katie leaps to her feet and dashes across the room. She peeks out the peephole, and relaxes as she sees Billie Susan from the diner standing there. She glances around and sees the woman is alone, and just as paranoid as she is. Katie opens the door and closes it quickly after Billie Susan pushes her way in.

"Lock it," she hisses.

Katie obeys and takes one more look out. Just an empty street meets her gaze. She's glad that this hotel has two stories but sad that it's in Elkins. What can you expect from a town with a population under seven hundred. It's almost as small as the town she's from.

"Sorry about all the cloak and dagger, but you have to

understand, Beverly is a very small town. We thrive on tourism, but we still don't want people asking too many questions that aren't Revolutionary or Civil War information," her southern drawl is a little thicker than Katie recalls but she understands.

Katie nods.

"That house ain't exactly in Beverly. You can get there from Beverly but … " she sighs.

"Something tells me that there's a reason I was watching Wrong Turn 4 just now."

Billie Susan chuckles and slaps her thigh. "You big city people are so funny. Making us all sound like we all hicks."

"No, ma'am, that isn't what I mean at all. It's just my brother wasn't exactly the nicest guy, and I can't even imagine him in West Virginia."

Katie takes a seat on the bed, and Billie Susan grabs up the desk chair.

"The problem is that your brother doesn't really own that house. My guess is he had some business with the real owners, and that isn't good. It has been rumored that the owners have either a meth lab or a moonshine still there, but it's so difficult to get to that location. Unless people start dropping like flies … it will remain as is … a mystery."

Katie sighs. *Drugs. Didn't brother die of an overdose?*

"From the look on your face something is clicking." Billie Susan leans back in the seat and drops off her shoes. She massages her big toe on her left foot. Her bunion is so large it could easily pass for a second big toe.

"Yeah, he died of a drug overdose. I couldn't tell you what kind as I have to be honest, my brother and I were on the outs. Our parents are not doing well. He always believed he was better than us. I'm actually from a small town about the size of Beverly. Maybe smaller." Katie stands and makes her way to the small refrigerator. "Would you like something to drink?"

"Sure, a soda would be good." Billie Susan drops her large purse on the floor and inhales deeply.

Katie hands Billie Susan a Coke. "I hope non diet is okay. I know that sounds silly, but so many people drink that diet crap. I just don't believe them."

"Thanks, no worries. I ain't cotton to diet either. Shit, I work twelve hours a day, six days a week. I need the sugar." Billie Susan pops the top and takes a long slug.

Katie takes her seat and opens her own can. "So what are you trying to tell me? I mean about the place?"

"The only way you can get to the cabin is with a jeep, and someone who knows their way around those backwoods. Otherwise … "

"I'll be someone's lunch?"

Billie Susan chuckles and shakes her head. "I don't think there are any cannibals out there, but then I don't spend a lot of time out there. Nobody is going to come at you with a chainsaw if that is what you fear."

Katie sighs. "Sorry, Wrong Turn 4 was on the television."

Billie Susan snickers. "I will tell you, there are some people out there who would rather shoot you than talk to you."

"You're going to think I'm crazy, but I get the feeling we need to go out there," Katie voices. Her heart skips a beat, pulsating up to her brain. She sniffs and takes a drink. Her eyes never leave the stranger in her room.

Billie Susan sighs. "I'm fifty-five-years-old. I was born and raised in Beverly. My family has a place not too far off from where that cabin is. Of course, I ain't lived there in over thirty years, but I heard a lot of rumors and such. What I do know is something is driving me to take you up there. I think the sooner we go, the better."

Katie's heart and mind race. *This could be a trap. Maybe she's part of the group. Oh hell, what am I saying? This is nuts. I have to see this place. I have to.*

"Oh, and another thing, you know how to use a gun?" Billie Susan asks.

+++

Staring down at the body of the father of my child, I don't know whether to cry or laugh. I reach out and touch his cheek. It's cold and lifeless but soft. "How did he die?"

"I haven't got the tox screen back, but from what I can tell, drug overdose. He and his partner were mules. I found several drug filled rubbers in both of them. Apparently one or two ruptured in their bellies." Carolyn turns to Olivia. "I should have the full report ready for you tomorrow."

"Did they have family to contact?" I step back. I try to look away but I can't. He looks exactly like the picture I made in my journal.

"Yes, as a matter-of-fact we found him in the system. Their families are pretty poor, so I'm not sure they'll be able to bring either of them back for a funeral."

"I'll pay," I remark.

"Shoshana," Deborah gasps, and races to me. She wraps her arms around my shoulders, as Noah makes his way to stand in front of me.

"Are you sure?" Noah asks.

"They are still people, aren't they? He was the father of my child. My only child. Something must have happened in that cabin otherwise I wouldn't be here." I gasp and gaze over at Olivia.

"Are you remembering something?" Olivia asks.

"I think the woman," I push through Deborah and Noah, and make my way to the other slab. I pull down the sheet and reveal Candy Sue's face. "Mickey and Candy Sue, they were with me in that cabin all right. Candy Sue could read but Mickey couldn't. She brought me the journals. She left me the map. The map … I think I left it in the cabin."

+++

Maddy stares into the darkness and shakes her head. *No, I don't even know what state I'm in. I don't know that I would even be out in the dark roaming around even if I was in Texas.* She sighs. "Okay, Baby Girl, right before the sun comes up we are going to take a little adventure."

+++

Mr. Zander opens the door and holds it for Mr. Big as he makes his way back into the office.

Mr. Big strolls toward the large plate, big bay windows and

stares down at the small crowd
dispersing in the open air
corridor. "Good, good, they are
all leaving. Did you give the
press the written statement?"

"Yes, sir, everyone received
a copy and I've made the
necessary appointments. Your
first one is after lunch."

"Uh huh," he sighs and
slides out of his jacket. Handing
it to Mr. Zander, he ambles over
to his desk. "How many loose ends
are closing?"

Mr. Zander hesitates.
"Almost all of them."

Mr. Big eyes the tall man,
he pulls a cigar from his humidor
and hands it to Mr. Zander.

Mr. Zander takes out his
cigar cutter and nips the ends.
He hands it back to Mr. Big.

"I told you, they clean up
nicely, didn't I?"

Mr. Zander nods as he stares
down at the cigar cutter. He
doesn't say a word.

"Who's left?" Mr. Big places the cigar in the corner of his mouth, gripping it tightly in his teeth.

Mr. Zander grins. "I believe there are two left."

"Can they connect me?"

"I don't believe so, sir."

"Is my wife here?"

"Yes, sir, would you like me to bring her in?"

Mr. Big stares toward the window and nods.

CHAPTER THIRTY-FIVE

Maddy wraps up the baby as warm as she possibly can, and straps her into the makeshift cradleboard. She straps it across her belly. Most are strapped on the woman or man's back, but if she did that then she wouldn't be able to put the backpack on. The backpack carries their supplies. *I want us to escape, not just die in the middle of God knows where of need.*

She slips the backpack onto her back and guesses she's now at least forty to fifty pounds heavier. She sighs and shakes her head. "I can do it. I can do it. No, we can do it. I have faith." Isn't that what the old preachers used to try to push into her brain seconds before they would shove their cocks into her mouth?

She frowns and gasps. "Ugh! Baby Girl, that's never going to happen to you, I promise." She's glad she put the stuff on after she made her way down the stairs otherwise she would never make it with that load.

Maddy gazes around the room, searching for anything that she might have missed. She feels for the map in her pocket before putting on the heavy duty work gloves she had found in the shed. "Okay world, ready or not, here we come. Okay, God, now you get to laugh."

***

Katie eases herself down on the toilet and sighs. *What the hell am I getting myself into? Please be the right thing, please be the right thing.*

"Are you okay?" Billie Susan asks.

"Yeah, I'm good," Katie answers.

Ten minutes later, Katie takes the shotgun out of the passenger seat, as they climb into Billie Susan's jeep.

Katie's stomach turns and she's glad she has her nausea medicine. She gazes into the back seat and frowns. It looks like an arsenal back there.

"Are you okay?" Billie Susan asks.

Katie chuckles. "I lived my whole life in a small town. Never really went anywhere more than the couple of years in college, and here I am on a wild goose chase in the middle of nowhere. Life sure is changing for me."

Billie Susan chuckles. "Girlfriend, this ain't no wild goose chase. This is real life. I don't know what I'm feeling, but it's stronger than ever."

"Do you think we've been flying under the radar?"

"Huh?" Billie Susan asks.

"I don't know." Katie shudders and pulls her jacket tightly around her shoulders. She sighs and swipes the sweat beads from her forehead.

"Are you all right?"

"I don't know. I just keep seeing a young woman and a baby. I think they are in danger."

Billie Susan inhales deeply and lets the used air slowly leave her lungs. "There's something I need to tell you."

"What?"

"The people that own that cabin are dead."

Katie gasps and clutches the seat, as she turns toward Billie Susan. "What the hell are you talking about?"

"I got the call last night. They's in New York City, dead. That's one of the reasons I decided I had to take you to the cabin. I was going to come to you last night to convince you to turn around and go home. But then I got the same feeling you did, yesterday before I left home."

+++

Mr. Big gazes up as the door opens, and the tall blonde with deep blue eyes strolls in. Her long blonde hair cascades over her white fox fur coat. Her five inch hooker heels make her look like a giant.

"You rang, Big Daddy?" Her full red lips reveal pearly white teeth.

"Mr. Zander?" Mr. Big calls out.

"Yes, sir," Mr. Zander closes the door and locks it.

"Take my wife's coat," he hisses.

"But Big Daddy, I thought we would be alone," she pouts, as she pulls the coat tighter about her thin shoulders.

Mr. Big stares at the woman who has been his wife these last two years. Amanda Blakely from Huntington, New Jersey. She almost won Miss New Jersey except she slept with the wrong judge.

"Take Baby Doll's coat, Mr. Zander," Mr. Big hisses.

Amanda gulps loudly as tears streak down her face. Baby Doll is the name she used when she worked as an exotic dancer a hundred years ago. She slides the coat off and lets it fall.

Mr. Zander reaches it before it hits the floor, and takes it over to the coat rack.

Amanda stares down at the red nylons streaming up her long

tanned legs to the red g-string and garter belt. The red heart bra accentuates her double Ds, thrusting them out to hard peaks pushing through the thin material. Her hands are at her sides. She isn't even sure what she should cover up.

"Ah, tears are going to smear your makeup. We can't have that, can we?"

She swipes at her cheeks and tries to muster a grin.

"Why are you crying?"

Amanda shakes her head and stares at the floor.

Mr. Big is on his feet, and standing in front of her in a flash. He snags his hand into her hair, and pulls her face up to his. "What the fuck were you thinking, cunt?"

"I'm so sorry, Big Daddy. I never meant to do anything. I swear. I just went to the club like you asked. Ordered my usual appletini, and after I drank it I felt funny," she whispers.

"I know. How many men you think you fucked last night?"

She gasps and shakes her head. "No, Big Daddy, I would never do that. I just found a corner and went to sleep. I didn't have sex with anyone. I haven't since we married."

"Baby Doll, you are lucky I'm feeling generous. I'm going to be running for political office soonest, and I can't have you showing up at some hospital or morgue. You're going to do something for me," Mr. Big whispers into her ear.

She sniffs and stares at the wall behind him. She doesn't dare move or risk his wrath.

He slips his free hand between her trembling thighs.

Her heart skips a beat, and she licks her lips. *Oh God, what did his goons do to me? All I did was go to the club and have a drink. Oh God, I didn't have sex with anyone. Please, God, tell him I didn't. Oh God, I'm gonna cum on his hand.*

"Mr. Zander."

Pulling a camcorder from his pocket, Mr. Zander walks over to Amanda.

Mr. Big releases his hold on her.

Her knees buckle beneath her, and she drops on the ground.

Mr. Zander turns it on, and shoves it in her face.

She gasps as she stares into the small screen. Tears streak down her face once more, and she's glad she is wearing waterproof mascara. She tries to look away, but Mr. Big shoves her face back.

She's wearing the outfit from last night. She watches as her best friend Angel, another leggy blonde, brings her to an orgasm on the table in the middle of the club. Soft sobs wrack her body and she wishes she could crawl under the carpet. A shiver races up and down her spine, as she realizes that not only was she drugged, but she was set up.

*Oh God, it's true what they say,
he really is a freak. Oh God,
please don't let him kill me.
I'll do anything, just please
don't let him kill me.*

Seconds later, a tall well
endowed man takes her friend's
mouths place. Squeezing her
eyelids shut, she can't stop the
image of the man shoving his big
penis into her. Her screams echo
from the camera into the room.

"I always told you if you
ever did anything like this there
would be a price to pay." Mr. Big
grins as he shoves her sobbing
body against the carpet. "I can't
kill you but I can sure as hell
make your life a living hell, now
can't I?"

+++

"You aren't going to do
something stupid and go to that
damn cabin, are you?" Deborah
asks, as we enter the apartment.

I make my way to the
bassinet in the living room.
Putting the baby carrier on the

couch, I pick up Chanah and hug her tightly against me.

Noah grabs the carrier and takes it to the corner where I keep it.

"I don't know." I lean down to kiss the baby's soft cheeks.

"Well, that would be insane. Noah, please tell her how crazy that sounds."

"I hardly think he's going to be a threat to me now, after all he's dead."

"What about the woman? You said she saved you," Noah voices.

"Yes, she did. She said she didn't want to be an Anne Wilkes, but she had read all of my books. She said someone paid them to take me, but she couldn't tell me who. He was mad. He didn't read or write. I can't believe how much I'm remembering. She's asleep so if you two don't mind, I'm off to the computer."

Deborah shrugs. "Are you going to stick around, Noah? I

think I'm needing some time with my husband."

I grin at her. "You know what, sister? I think that sounds like a great idea. I know he and the children visit often but I'm guessing you need a little time with your husband. Take your time. I'm sure we'll be fine."

Deborah giggles. "If I didn't know better I would swear you're trying to get rid of me."

"Seriously, it has been over a month or so since you've been home. Go … go before I decide I need you. I should be safe."

Deborah races to her room before I have a chance to say more.

"Are you sure?" Noah asks, as he makes his way toward me. He wraps his arms around me and pulls me closer.

"If you'll just stay until I get some work done, I think I'll be fine."

Noah nods. "It's all coming back, isn't it?"

I nod and gaze toward the baby. My heart skips a beat and a shiver races up and down my spine as I think about my time away from home. *How did I get away? I memorized the map the woman gave me, but that still doesn't tell me how I actually executed the escape. Oh God, I know I should be thrilled that I'm at least remembering this much but really … I have a feeling I need to have instant recall right now.*

CHAPTER THIRTY-SIX

"She's right, isn't she?" Noah asks, as he comes back in after helping Deborah out.

"About what?" I pick up Chanah and kiss her forehead.

She nuzzles me.

"Right about what?" Placing Chanah in the football position, I pull up my blouse.

"You're going to the cabin, aren't you?" He grins and plops down in the easy chair. His dark eyes never leave mine. His Cheshire cat smirk spreads wider across his face.

Sticking out my tongue, I blow him a raspberry or as we say in New York, a "Bronx cheer".

"I know that you feel you should do the right thing."

"Right now the right thing is to find the bastards who kidnapped me. You saw the video surveillance tapes. That giant in the morgue couldn't be either one. I can't exactly ask Stan because he's dead. So what else is there left for me?"

"Well, I have to admit when you said you wanted to pay to have them taken back to their homes. I was worried. I figured you would ask to ride in the back of the ambulance or hearst, or whatever they transport bodies in." He chuckles and eyes the ceiling. "You're definitely one of a kind."

"Well, I do have the baby to think about. Can you get a car? I've already checked to see how long it would take." I sigh. Already my mind is racing to what all I will need to pack. I've never travelled with a baby before, this will be a huge adventure.

"Sure, what are we going to tell your sister?"

"That I need a few days in the country."

***

Katie glances in the back seat as they leap into the older model Jeep. *I can't believe I'm doing this. I don't know this woman. She has a bag of guns and bullets, as well as a bow and quiver full of very sharp arrows. Oh, shit, I've done it now.* Facing the windshield, she slides the seatbelt over her shoulder and hooks it. *There's no turning back now.*

"I know what you're thinking," Billie Susan voices.

"No, I don't think you do." Katie watches the sun peek through the dark clouds, as pinks and purples dance in the sky.

"About now you're thinking 'what have I got myself into?'. Am I right?"

Katie nods as they make their way toward the highway and the complete unknown.

"I don't blame you. I'm scared too and I know this area. I know these people."

"Why the arsenal?"

"Just because some of these are my relatives, doesn't mean I'm well liked by all of them."

+++

"What do you mean we're going to West Virginia?" Kevin glares at Olivia.

"You know damn well why we're going to West Virginia."

"Because we're expendable? Collateral damage for the government? Why can't they do this if they're so worried?"

Olivia sneers at her partner. She supposes that if she had a family she would be more careful too. "I'm sorry. If you want to back out, I would understand."

Kevin sighs and stares at the picture of his wife and children. "This case reminds me of why I became a cop. When they made me detective ten years ago I thought 'wow, I'm in the big leagues now', but then everything slowed down because of the children. I don't resent my wife's career but sometimes it has held me back. I kept telling myself, 'She's a doctor. She saves lives every day, and I'm lucky to catch a perv with his dick hanging out.'"

"And now?"

"I love finding the clues on the bodies. For once, when I go home I'm wondering how the clues go together. I love my job."

"So, are you ready to go to West Virginia?"

Pulling the backpack out from under the desk, he grins. "Ready when you are."

CHAPTER THIRTY-SEVEN

Staring out the window, I frown. "Noah, what the hell is that pulling up? Looks like a freaking tank."

Noah chuckles and shakes his head. "I swear, I ordered us an earth friendly car."

Olivia and Kevin jump out of the front seats, and make their way toward us.

The Doorman steps up and opens the door for them.

"What's going on?" I eye them before glaring back at Noah who's still smirking in my direction.

"We'll explain on the way. We already have the car seat set up in the back," Kevin grabs up my diaper bag and small case and tosses them in the back as well as Noah's small valise.

"Watch the place," I half heartedly call to the doorman but already I know he will. I climb in and snap the baby in before applying my own seatbelt.

Minutes later, we're on the road and fighting the morning traffic already beginning to build up.

"Have you read a newspaper lately?" Olivia asks.

"No, not really. Should I?"

Noah hands me the morning paper.

Opening it up, I gasp as I stare at the familiar face on the cover. "I know this man."

"You knew that man," Noah corrects.

"What do you mean?" The baby sneezes just as I'm about to glance at the headline. Pulling a cloth diaper from my coat pocket, I swipe the goo from her nose and mouth.

"I'll take care of her, you read." Noah takes the rag from my hand and coos to the baby. She grins at him.

Glancing back down at the newspaper, I frown.

> **Honors Funeral held today for New York's own beloved Ted George. He set a new record in convictions for sex offenders and child abusers. He will surely be missed.**

"What the hell? I know I've seen this man before," I gasp.

"Well, he was in the newspaper and on television all the time. How could you miss him?" Olivia asks.

I snicker. "You have to understand, I stopped watching the news and reading the newspapers a few years before I disappeared. All the depressing news was just shutting me down. It seemed like everywhere I looked there were lies and tribulations. I needed to be positive to write."

"To write horror?" Noah sniggers.

I lovingly shove his shoulder. "You, but seriously," I sigh, "I just didn't pay attention, but I do know this face." Grabbing up the diaper bag, I pull the baggie covered journal out. I take it out and rummage through the pages finally stopping on one. Handing the book to Kevin, I pick up the newspaper and gaze back down at it. *Yeah, I know that face all right.*

"It's him all right," Kevin answers. He shows it to Olivia as we wait at the light.

"What did he have to do with it?" Olivia asks.

"I still don't remember the men who kidnapped me from the hospital, but he came to the place where they kept me at first. At least that's what the journal says. Last night I had a dream." I shudder as a shiver races up and down my spine.

It's all I can do to keep from screaming. Tears form in the corners of my eyes. A soft sob escapes my lips as I stare down at my baby. It's all I can do to keep from snatching her up and leaping from the car. Where would I run to?

"Shoshana?" Noah reaches for my hand.

"I'm sorry. I guess I'm just tired. I didn't get much sleep last night. That man might have been a big hero to New York City, but he isn't a hero to me."

+++

Maddy steps into the garage and looks around. *You would think that with as large a garage this is that there would be at least one old car in here that I could hotwire.* Shaking her head, she sighs and heads back out. The temperature is a little cooler than it was a few minutes ago. She starts making her way down the snow covered road. She's glad the snow's just a light dusting.

How many times did Shoshana take this road before she finally made it out? Oh God, please don't let us freeze to death before we make it out.

+++

"What were they doing out there?" Katie asks, as she picks up her cup of coffee and lets it warm her cool hands. What a great time to forget gloves.

Billie Susan chuckles. "I don't want to add to the stereotypical life of mountain folk, but I guarantee it wasn't anything legal."

"And you say no one comes this way because of the dangers?" Katie asks.

"You would have to know the area to get in and out safely. Even with helicopters it's pretty risky. You'll see as we get closer." Billie Susan reaches into the door side pocket, and pulls out a pair of gloves. She hands them to Katie.

"Thank you." Katie takes them after she puts the cup back in the cup holder. She slips them on and grins. They are fur lined and warm. "I know I probably sound like a country bumpkin asking so many questions. Back home they found a serial killer about twenty miles into the country. The only reason they found him was because one of his victims escaped. It was awful. The things he did to her. She killed herself right after he was sentenced. I guess she waited long enough to see if justice would be served."

"And the serial killer?"

"He'll be out in 2036."

Billie Susan's eyes widen as she glances at her new friend.

"Nah, just kidding but the way politicians play fast and loose with some of these killers, you never know. We don't have the death penalty. The governor repealed it some years ago. Said it was wrong and that too many were being killed, so now we get to keep them locked up eating food good people need. Giving 'em health care that poor people can't have and don't even get me started on how much it costs to house them." Katie sighs.

Billie Susan chuckles. "Whew, for a minute there I feared I was with one of them liberals that didn't believe in self-defense or killing when you need to."

Katie shakes her head. "That ain't me, sister. One of the reasons my brother and I were on the outs was because I heard he was into some pretty messed up stuff." She shudders.

"Like what?"

Her voice lowers despite the fact they're alone. "I found a DVD amongst his stuff in a locked box. I guess he came to my parents' house while I wasn't there. Anyway," she sighs, "I saw … " she gasps and shudders again.

"What did you see?" Billie Susan slows down and pulls the Jeep over to the shoulder, and turns toward Katie.

Tears race down Katie's cheeks, she shivers and sobs. "Oh God, he was raping a young girl and then … " she gasps.

Billie Susan reaches for the woman's shoulders and pulls her toward her.

Katie sobs violently against the other woman's arms. "He beat her. He and a woman cut her up. She was still alive when they started. They were laughing the whole time like it was a game. A game?"

"Sh … it's going to be okay. Your brother is dead. He can't hurt any more girls," Billie Susan whispers.

Katie sniffles and nods. "I didn't know whether to burn the stuff or what. Right now it's in his room. I guess none of it matters now. He's dead. I have no idea who that woman was. I tried to watch the news to see if I saw anything. Missing persons and all. Nothing."

"I suspect if you give the DVD to the police, they might know who she is," Billie Susan answers.

Katie pulls away and sighs. She reaches into her pocket and pulls out a Kleenex. Swiping at her nose and mouth, she stares into the other woman's eyes.

"That's why you came here, isn't it? To see if she is here? Or maybe some other victims?" Billie Susan pushes Katie's hair from her eyes.

Katie nods. "It was awful."

Billie Susan sighs. "I know that cabin well enough to know that if something horrible was going to happen around here that would definitely be the place it would happen at."

CHAPTER THIRTY-EIGHT

Tears stream down my cheeks, I reach up to swipe them off but can't move my arms. *Why the hell can't I see? Where the hell am I?* It takes me a minute to realize that my arms are tied down and that I'm lying on an old army cot. Every muscle in my body aches and I bite my tongue to keep from screaming.

I listen intently to the silence.

I tug on my feet. They're tied down as well.

A knock on the door catches my attention.

Moving my head back and forth, I find the cloth covering my eyes moves. A flash of a hundred rats' nests building up in my hair crosses my mind before I consider the fact I want to see where I am. *Where the hell am I?* I sigh softly.

"Yeah," a soft male voice answers, as he opens the door.

"I got the stuff. Is she still out?" the stronger male voice asks.

"Oh yeah, I'd say give her another day and we can remove the ropes. She'll be begging us for this shit. It's that fucking good."

Two more pushes and bingo! Through small slits, I stare at the two backs.

One man is dressed in a dark expensive suit. His black hair is thick but not long. He glances my way and grins. "How long before I can have a little fun with her?"

The younger man turns around. "You want to fuck that? Man, with all the women you get, I would think she'd be a little too old for you." His emo hair falls into his eyes, as he takes the small brown package from the older man.

The older man steps toward me. He grips my naked breast and

squeezes. "I need her now, mother fucker. Fix her up."

The younger man takes his place in a lawn chair across from me. He opens the small package and lays it on an antique TV dinner tray. He drops some white powder into a spoon.

I close my eyes and try not to think about what's about to happen to me. *Drugs. Drugs? Oh, God, no, why did they have to give me drugs? What is that asshole about to do to me?* I peek through the slit again, and stare at the man's hand gripping my forearm.

He holds the syringe in his mouth as he searches for a vein. Finally finding one, he takes the syringe from his mouth and glides the needle into my arm.

I gasp as the drug slowly makes its way into my vein, pulsating against my heart and brain. It almost feels like my brain will explode, almost. *Oh God, please let me be all right. Please.*

The young man removes the blindfold and lightly slaps my cheeks. "We got company, bitch."

I open my eyes as wide as I can, as my heart skips a beat before taking off like a horse running the Kentucky Derby. *God, I frigging hope my horse comes in. if it doesn't, I want a refund on this dope.* I glance over at the older man and gasp. He's naked and standing at the foot of the cot.

"Untie her," he hisses.

The younger man obeys.

Reaching down, I push myself up to a sitting position. My hands tremble against the cot, and for a second I think I'm going to fall over, but I don't.

"That's good. It looks like you're ready for your lunch. I hope you have a good appetite because I got a lot to feed you." He steps over some trash on the floor, and stands before me. Grabbing my ears, he tries to shove my mouth onto his waiting member.

I arch my back and try to pull away. Pain sears through my ears as I shake my head. "Fuck you," I hiss.

"You do what I fucking want you to do or you die," he whispers.

My knees hit my chest and I slam my feet into his erection, knocking him backward.

"What the fuck? Get that bitch," he hisses.

Emo boy grabs my arms and shoves me against the wall. He slams my body into the wall once more.

Stars flash through my eyes, as my head hits the wall a second time. I sniff and pick up the scent of Old Spice and ammonia. Bile rises up the back of my throat, and I fight the urge to vomit. If I were watching television the woman in the scene would probably spit on the man, but not me.

My knees wobble beneath me and hit the floor. "Oh God," I whisper.

The older man returns once more. He grins. "Oh yeah, she's ready. "

Emo boy stands behind me. Holding my arms behind my back, he leans into my spine forcing me to pop out my breasts toward the other man's face.

The older man shoves his hard penis into my open mouth and I try to scream, as I stare into the man's eyes. Big brown evil eyes. I scream.

"Shoshana, wake up!" a familiar voice calls from a tunnel somewhere off in space.

"Shoshana," a soft female voice whispers.

A baby cries in the background.

"No!" I scream. "Leave me the fuck alone!" I try to slap at the hands around me but I can't. They are held down at my side. "Please stop!"

"Shoshana, it's Noah. Please come back, please come back."

"Sweetie, come on, come back to us," the female voice whispers again.

I open my eyes and gasp. My heart skips a beat as I glance between the three pairs of staring eyes. "Where am I?"

Noah squeezes my hand as Olivia caresses my cheek.

"Are you all right?" Kevin asks.

"Where am I?"

"You're in a car. We're on our way to West Virginia. Are you okay?" Olivia asks.

I sigh. "What happened?"

"I think you fell asleep," Noah answers.

"That man … in my dream," I reach for Chanah and put the pacifier back in her mouth.

She accepts it and stares into my eyes. She sighs and kicks.

"I'm sorry, baby. I'm sorry." Tears fill my eyes, I try to keep them focused but I can't. "I'm so sorry." The tears flow down my cheeks. "That man, the one in the picture … he raped me and beat me. He kept me drugged until they took me to Mickey's. I don't know how I can even remember that. I tried to get away a couple of times. Right after the last attempt was when they took me to Mickey. I don't remember a lot but something about a book and how it was going to make him look bad, but I have no idea what book." I sniffle and reach for the handkerchief in Kevin's hand.

Olivia sighs and stares back at the road.

No one says a word, as Kevin pulls the vehicle back on the road.

+++

Mr. Big stares out the plate glass window.

Mr. Zander pours a large highball and brings it to the older man.

Mr. Big takes it and downs it. "Next time, less ice and ginger ale."

Mr. Zander returns with the next drink.

Mr. Big sighs and takes it. "I don't know."

"Sir?"

"Why the hell didn't Ole Mickey kill her? He kills all of them, but not her."

"From what he told me, he fell in love."

"You actually talked to that big ass mother fucker?"

Mr. Zander coughs and stares at his feet. "Yes, sir."

"What about the newest girl?"

"He said she was dead, or at least that's what they told me he said minutes before he died."

"What the fuck? What if that bitch remembers everything? What the hell? Do I have to take care of everything? Get my car ready, looks like we're going to have to make a road trip."

+++

Maddy grabs the wagon handle and trudges back down the road. Looking backward, she shakes her head and frowns. *I've gone what, a hundred yards from the house?* Her legs burn from the tops of her thighs down to the tips of her toes.

She inhales deeply, but the air burns deep inside her lungs. She gasps and shakes her head. "I have to do this. I have to get out. If Shoshana could do this, then so can I." She closes her eyes and pushes forward.

The next time she glances back, the house is but a dot. She grins. "Just keep walking, just keep walking."

+++

Billie Susan gazes through the trees and frowns. Slowing down, she stares at the road ahead of them.

Katie reaches for the small bow and arrow set. It might be small, but she's pretty sure it's mighty. She knocks an arrow, holding it tight in her left hand, she rolls down the window with her right.

Billie Susan flips off the music, as she eyes the road around them.

Something flits across the right side of the car.

Katie rests the curvature of the bow out the window and gazes around them. *This is silly, I'm just seeing shadows in the dark, but it isn't dark, is it?* Katie doesn't blink. She scans the area once more and sighs as she pulls the bow back into the Jeep.

"I think it was just the wind."

"I don't know. I've never seen the wind wear a protective orange vest before."

CHAPTER THIRTY-NINE

I spy the helicopter overhead and frown. *We ain't in Kansas anymore.* "Does that have anything to do with us?"

Olivia giggles. "We could only hope. Let's put it this way, if it is, they didn't tell us about it."

I nod and watch as it takes off in the opposite direction. I sigh. "You guys never did tell me why you're coming with me. I'm pretty sure Beverly, West Virginia isn't in your jurisdiction." My cell rings, interrupting my thought. Glancing at the cell, I frown. It's my sister. "Hello, Deborah."

"Please tell me you aren't headed toward West Virginia."

"Okay, I won't tell you. Did Noah leave a message for you to feed the cat?"

"Damnit, how the hell am I going to keep you safe when you jump right into the mouth of the beast?"

"Deborah, did you vote for Ted George?"

She hesitates and sighs. "What are you talking about?"

"We do vote for DA, don't we?"

"Yes."

"Well, did you vote for him?"

She sighs. "Why are you asking?"

"Because he was one of the asswipes who held me captive. I don't think he took me from the hospital, but I do know he was the one giving them drugs to feed me. He raped me."

"B-u-u-t-t I thought you couldn't remember anything."

"I didn't until today. Well, I didn't remember the first time in New York before going to the cabin, but now … I don't recall everything … I just know that he tried to kill me."

She sighs. "Are you okay?"

"Yeah, I'll be okay." I hit the mute button and turn toward Olivia. "What if these monsters decide to come after me and my family?"

Glancing toward the newspaper, Olivia nods toward Kevin. "I'm on it." She slides her cell from her pocket.

"Deborah, are you at home?"

"No, I'm at your home."

"Was there an officer at the door when you came through?"

"No, and that's why I thought it was strange. As soon as I came up and saw the car seat gone, I knew. What are you trying to find?"

"I don't know, but please don't leave until a police officer comes to the house. Can you do that?" I stare at Olivia and she nods.

"Okay, I will stay but please, please be very careful. Okay?"

I nod as I speak into the receiver. "Okay."

"Now let me speak to Noah," she booms into the phone so loudly I have to pull it away from my ear. "She wants to speak to you."

Noah sticks out his tongue and showers me with a "Bronx" cheer.

I giggle and shake my head.

+++

"Are you sure we shouldn't fly?" Mr. Zander asks, as he pours another highball.

"We would only attract attention," Mr. Big answers.

"So the extra long piece of shit limo isn't going to do that?"

Mr. Big glares at the younger man.

Mr. Zander drops his chin to his chest. "I'm sorry, sir. I didn't mean that. I know you can do all things. You're like a god to those of us who work for you."

"You better fucking believe it too. If you ever talk like that to me again, with or without an audience … I promise you will be an example to all the others of what not to do."

Mr. Zander sighs. Turning his back to Mr. Big, he pops open his round cufflink top, and drops the white powder into the whiskey. Stirring it lightly with the tip of his finger, he smiles as it instantly dissolves. He hands it back to the large man, and watches him gulp it down like a glass of water.

Mr. Big sighs and rests his head on the back of the soft leather. He closes his eyes and drops the empty glass on the floorboard.

Mr. Zander snatches it up, opens the window and tosses it from the moving car. It smashes against the ground as the car speeds down the road.

+++

Deborah grabs the tent and kicks it across the room. It flies and smacks against the wall, spilling the contents on the floor. She sighs and strolls over to right it and take it back to the other corner when the buzzer rings. She makes her way to the one next to the elevator. "Hello."

"NYPD, ma'am we're supposed to make sure you're safe," the male voice calls into the speaker downstairs.

Deborah sighs. *Yeah, this is what my life has become.* "Okay, come on up." Deborah glances around the foyer and stares at the ugly, nasty tent. She flips it upright and starts tossing the fallen goods back into the open tent flap. She picks up the small penknife as the elevator doors slide open. Without thinking, she slides it into the hem of her pants, as her heart skips a beat.

Out of the corner of her eye, she spots two large men racing toward her. The larger one grabs her by the waist as the smaller one pulls a syringe from his pocket.

She screams and kicks at the stranger's hands, as he pins her arm against the bigger man.

Both men wear NYPD uniforms with obscure badges.

"Get the fuck away from me, you scumbugs. You'll never get away with this," she hisses.

The man in front of her grins, as he kisses her cheek and slides the needle into a vein. "Are you sure we can't have a little fun with this one?"

"The boss man says she is all his," the other one answers. "You know how he likes 'em untouched."

"Yeah, yeah, whatever."

+++

Billie Susan slows down even more, as she dodges something rolling on the ground.

"What the hell is on the road?"

Billie Susan grins. "I'm guessing it's something to slow down the unwanted. They would come crashing down this road and not see them. I wouldn't with the light layer of snow if I didn't know about it."

Katie nods. She catches something else skitter in the trees. "Okay, this is the third time I've seen something flashing in those woods. Am I losing my mind, or what?"

"Or what is more than likely. I told you they got scouts in this area. I got a few kin that just ain't happy unless they living like 'real mountain men', whatever the hell that is. As far as I can see that means not settling down and working a real job like most of us. They live in long cabins on their grandparents or even great-grandparents land and some don't have electricity. I guess they do nicely after all. They ain't worried about the internet failing or their favorite television programs."

Katie sighs. *Yeah, I think there might be something to not having to worry about all that.* She sighs again and stares back out the window.

+++

Olivia's phone rings and she picks it up on the second ring. "Yo."

"Did you say the sister is at Shoshana Meyers' house?"

"Yes, why? Aren't you there?"

"Well, we're here now. We had to get the doorman to let us in. The foyer is a mess, and the sister's purse is still here. We have searched the whole place, and she isn't here. What should we do?"

Olivia sighs. "Put out an APB. I don't think they've gone to far."

I sit up and stare at the back of Olivia's head. "What's going on with my sister?"

Noah grabs my arm and pulls me back.

I push forward, ignoring him. My heart skips a beat and a sinking feeling hits the pit of my stomach. *Oh God, what if I have put my sister's life in danger? No, God, please let her be okay. Please let her be okay.*

"Yeah, uh huh, okay."

"What's going on?" I grab the back of Olivia's seat again and pull backward. "Please tell me it is another case."

Olivia and Kevin share a quick glance.

Olivia sighs and turns back to me. She clicks the phone off. "It's going to be all right. They're going to find her. The doorman got the license plate number so they should be easy to find."

Tears fill my eyes as I think about my sister. She's strong, but I don't know if she's as strong as me. *I just can't believe those asswipes would take my sister. Were they looking for me again? What are they going to do with her? Oh God, please don't let them hurt her. Please.*

CHAPTER FORTY

The smell of ammonia fills her nostrils before she's completely awake. The heat of the overhead lights burn into her eyes making it almost impossible to open them. *What the hell is going on here? Where the hell am*

I? Oh, God, what a headache I have. She tries to rub her eyes and hears a clang as her arm is slammed back against the metal.

I'm lying on a metal cot. What am I doing on this metal cot? She searches her mind for the last thing she did before waking up here, wherever here is. *I was home with my husband and children. I told them I needed to go check on her. I took a taxi to her house. I kicked that damn tent. Two cops came up and ...* she gasps. *I'm guessing they weren't police.* She sighs.

Listening intently, she lets the warmth from the lights filter through to her brain, warming her despite the coldness of the room.

Silence greets her.

A knock at the door gets her attention.

"Yo," the young male voice says, as he opens the squeaking door.

"Hey, we got to move her." The other male voice is older, with a hint of an accent.

"She ain't woke up yet," the young man answers.

"It don't matter. We got to move her now. Someone made the plates and they's registered to

356

this place. She's probably awake. You got the lights on so bright ... mother fucker. You would never know you're a meth head with the fucking lights this bright, Jesus." The older man flips the switch and plunges them into semi-darkness.

Deborah sighs. She opens her eyes and takes a look around the room as she adjusts her eyes to her surroundings and semi-darkness. A simple room. Maybe even an old hotel room. She's on an army cot in the middle of the kitchenette. She bites her lip as she spies several small rats scurrying up the cabinet wall and diving into the sink filled with dirty dishes. *Oh God, please don't let those things come over here.* She tugs on her wrists and ankles and realizes it isn't rope she's tied down with but handcuffs.

"Let me get the blanket. We don't want people thinking we carry bodies around every day," older man voices.

Young man chuckles. "Do you even know where you are? People toting bodies all over the place here. No one ever says a word, but it would be easier to carry

357

her if we roll her up burrito style. Her sister was a real fighter. Fucker broke my nose and popped out two of my back teeth."

Deborah gasps and coughs. Try as she might to stifle the cough ... it breaks free.

"Get her," the older man states.

The younger man grabs something from the small table by his lawn chair and makes his way toward her.

Deborah opens her eyes as he sticks the needle in her arm. "Please don't," she whispers as the drug starts surging through her vein. She stares into the deepest green eyes she has ever seen and sighs.

The smile never leaves the young man's face.

+++

"Billie Susan, do you think they have any girls at the cabin now?" The question hangs in the air. It's the question that needed to be asked, but no one seemed to want to voice it.

"I don't know."

"Am I silly for wanting to know?"

Billie Susan shakes her

head. "That's part of the reason I'm headed out that way. Ole Mickey and Candy Sue worked with these guys you see glimpses of, but they weren't always on friendly terms. I shouldn't tell you this but a couple of years ago, no, more like twenty. Anyway, Ole Mickey got hisself a girl. He and another cousin were in there having their way with her when a couple of other cousins decided they wanted her."

Billie Susan frowns. "They, the jealous cousins, came storm trooping into the cabin and there was such a war. By the time they were done the place was in pretty bad shape. The dumbasses were still trying to rape the girl while they was shooting and fighting. I tell you ... almost makes me ashamed that they are kin. BUT as the saying goes ... you can pick your friends but not your kin."

Katie shudders and stares out the window. "That's good to know even if it does make my skin crawl. Girlfriend, I think we have some company." Katie points toward a four-wheeler riding parallel with their Jeep.

Billie Susan glances toward

it and shivers. "Get ready, that ain't one of the nice ones."

Katie grabs up the bow once more and prepares to fire it. Staring out the window, she struggles with whether it's better to roll it up or down. At least down she could have a good chance of getting them before they had her. She shudders at the thought of some big hillbilly trying to have sex with her while she's bleeding to death.

The green and brown vehicle almost hides behind the foliage even with the light layer of snow. Two riders and neither of them are small. One is glaring right at them. Shotguns in both hands. The driver seems oblivious to the rider and the Jeep, and trudges on toward the cabin.

"Do they even see us?" Katie asks.

"Oh, you can count on that one. They both saw us otherwise they wouldn't be down here. Virgil is the driver and Oliver is the rider. They are both some of the meanest bucks in this county outside of Ole Mickey, and something tells me they've already gotten wind that he's dead."

+++

"Can't we get there any faster?" I whisper to no one in particular. I'm normally relaxed but right now ... not so much.

"It's an eight hour drive. Please be patient," Olivia states, as she sighs.

"I'm sorry. I just feel like someone is in danger. I know that sounds crazy. I probably wouldn't be worried, but I keep thinking of my sister and the cabin. I know Mickey is dead. Who else would even think of taking her to that cabin?" My mind races back to Ted George and his picture in the newspaper. "About now I sure wish I was a mystery writer and not horror."

Noah chuckles. "I think with everything you've gone through, probably qualifies as horror, don't you think?"

I sigh and nod.

"Besides, NYPD will alert me as soon as they find your sister. It's only a matter of time."

"Oh my God, does her husband even know? This is going to make him and the children nuts." I pull the baby closer to me.

Noah folds his arm around my

shoulders. Cradling me and the baby closer to him, he kisses my forehead.

"The police are with them now. They even went to the schools and brought the children home. They didn't want to take any chances on this one. I had a long conversation with my chief while you were sleeping or should I say, having a nightmare." Olivia faces me. She tries to smile but only grimaces.

I sigh and nod. "That's good to know. I'm sorry I'm being so much trouble. I just don't know about my sister and the kidnappers. I mean I have no proof that they are the same ones, but I just don't know if she could handle it all."

"Apparently they are already on that. Comparing the DVDs from the hospital and the security cameras at your place, they seem to fit the same descriptions."

"Huh?" Kevin perks up as he eyes Olivia.

Olivia holds up her phone, showing a recent text.

He nods and returns his attention to driving.

"They'll drug her." Tears roll down my face, I want to cry

but I can't. I want to scream but I can't. All I can do is hold my baby against my body through our restraints, and pray that everything will come out all right.

+++

Maddy gazes around them and sighs. She turns back toward the house as she reaches a more leveled out road. It's hidden behind a small clump of trees. The ruts are gone and it's just a plain dirt road. She remembers this was in the journal as well. Pulling the water bottle out of the wagon, she takes a few quick sips before checking on the baby.

Her face aches as well as the rest of her body. *Guess I should have practiced carrying an extra forty pounds for days before I started this stunt.* "But then how was I to know they weren't coming back for me. Huh, Baby Girl? It looks like it's just you and me here."

She places the bottle of water back in the wagon and starts walking. It's easy to stop, but not so easy to restart. Her legs push through the pain, as her brain urges her forward.

+++

The four wheeler pulls off into the long thicket. The driver cuts off the engine and leaps off. He swipes the sweat film and dirt from his face. He's tall, at least six-seven, but light and limber unlike most of the menfolk in his family. Virgil slugs Oliver's arm before grabbing the other gun from the man's hand. "Looks like we got us a couple of live ones."

"I'll say. You know, I seen a lot of things in my time but I have rarely seen women going to Ole Mickey's place on their own accord. What do you suppose could be up?"

Virgil shrugs. "I don't know but I could use a good woman right now. Something tells me there be aplenty over there in that there cabin."

"Well, if you would be nice to 'em once in a while, they might just want to stick around," Oliver chuckles.

"You ain't exactly winning any prizes in the female department neither. I think the last time I saw you with a woman was when we chased those two up here. She was half dead when you was fucking her. I didn't hear her scream once. She just made that weird gurgling sound and went limp."

"Well, next time don't shoot her," Oliver growls.

"Then next time let me have the pick of the litter."

CHAPTER FORTY-ONE

Katie sighs and lets the bow hang at her side as the four wheeler disappears into the thicket. "Looks like we're safe for now."

"Don't get your hopes up, those guys don't give up easily. Something must be up," Billie Susan answers, as her eyes scan the horizon. She lets the Jeep pick up speed, but remains cautious against road mines.

+++

Mr. Big blinks twice before opening his eyes. *What the hell*

have those asswipes done now? He
sighs and gazes about him. His
large body is propped up on large
overstuffed pillows. He's lying
on a king size bed. *Why the hell
am I here? I'm supposed to be on
my way to West Virginia to make
sure those assholes haven't
screwed up the loose ends.* "Mr.
Zander!" he screams at the top of
his lungs.

Mr. Zander peeks his head in
the doorway. "Yes, Mr. Big?"

"Where the hell are we?" He
sits up and gazes around him. The
room is small with the bed taking
up much of the room and all of
the decor.

"You're in a camper on your
way to West Virginia," Mr. Zander
answers matter-of-factly.

"What the hell? Where is my
limo? You know I always ride in
style." He tries to stand but his
knees buckle under him, and he
drops back onto the bed.

"You are traveling in style.
This way you have a bathroom and
home cooked meals any time you
like. We don't have to stop for
anything. We get in and out
before anyone knows it."

Mr. Big frowns. "What the
hell is that supposed to mean."

Mr. Zander shrugs. "Don't you always say 'take the safest way, always, in and out and make it quick'?"

Mr. Big sighs again. "Yeah, that's me. Okay, how about a meal. I'm getting hungry about now."

Mr. Zander grins. "As you wish."

Mr. Big watches his right hand man shut the door before trying to stand again. "Damn, I can't believe I drank that much. I better watch that. Too easy to get caught up and sloppy."

+++

Deborah listens intently for a few minutes before she opens her eyes to take in her surroundings. Her mouth feels like it's stuffed full of cotton. *Probably from whatever they gave me. Dumb, stupid drugs.* She fights the urge to cough. *Not good to make noise until I know exactly where I am.* Finally, she opens her eyes, and spies a tall man in a dark suit flittering about the kitchen.

Scanning the room, she lets

her body sink into the soft cushions underneath her. Without warning, she sneezes twice. *Oh shit, that can't be good.*

"Bless you," the man states, as he faces her and winks.

"I," she tries to speak but her voice comes out barely above a whisper.

He places a finger to his upper lip and points toward a door.

She stops.

He picks up a small tray and disappears behind the door. He comes back several minutes later and makes his way toward her. Dropping to his knees beside her head, he pulls a blanket up about her shoulders. "Don't say a word," he whispers. "You'll find out everything soon enough."

"Why?"

He grins. Kissing the top of her head, he leaps to his feet and makes his way toward another door close to her head.

This is strange. This is very strange. I could go. I could leave right now and no one would know. Gripping the side of the small mattress, she pulls herself up. A small chain clangs against a metal base. She spots it before it clangs again. A small fetter wrapped around her right ankle dangles over the side of the mattress.

Oh, God, I'm never going to get out of this alive.

++++++

"Do our usual?" Oliver asks before they hop back on the four-wheeler.

Virgil grins and nods. He leaps back into the driver's seat and guns the engine.

Oliver takes his place, and pumps the .20 gauge shotgun in his left hand twice. Two chambers ... two shells filled with buckshot. Works very well on tires.

Katie cringes as the sound of the four wheeler reaches her ears. "Mother fucker." She rolls down the window and nocks the arrow once more.

"I told you they don't give up that easily. I'm guessing they suddenly realized we're girls." Billie Susan chuckles.

"But aren't you related to them?"

Billie Susan shakes her head. "These things are like pitbulls in heat. They would fuck each other if one of them had a vagina. I ain't saying they ever did any queer shit but I wouldn't be surprised. They could see me every day of my life, and still not realize I'm kin. Let's just hope we get to them before they get to us."

Katie nods as she spots the four-wheeler pull out ahead of them.

It barrels down the road toward them going twice as fast as Billie Susan's Jeep.

Katie aims for the right front tire, letting her body dangle from the window from the waist up. She holds her breath and lets the arrow fly.

The four-wheeler darts across the lane and swerves back seconds after Katie lets loose with the second arrow.

It slams into Virgil's right calf.

"Damn, and I'm guessing he's wearing boots thick enough to choke a mule."

Nocking another arrow, Katie aims again. She's thankful for all those summers at summer camp and hunting with her dad. She couldn't always eat the deer meat, but she never failed to pull one down with a heart shot when she wanted to.

The Jeep and four-wheeler are nose to nose within fifteen feet of each other.

Katie's brain pulsates against her skull, as she realizes what she must do seconds before she leaps up into the window and lets go of the next arrow.

The arrow slams into the right tire and rips through, pulling the four-wheeler to the right.

Oliver aims the shotgun at Katie as they pass one another seconds before he points it toward the Jeep's back tire and shoots.

The pop sounds like an explosion, as the back tire takes a direct hit and caves instantly.

Katie's heart skips a beat, as she slides back into the Jeep and holds onto the seatbelt for dear life.

The Jeep slides right and left, and right again before finally rolling over twice and landing upright in the middle of the field.

Katie gasps and holds her breath, as her parents' faces flash in her brain. *I'm sorry, Mom and Dad. Your daughter really is a total idiot. She died because she's as curious as a cat.* She spots her new friend out of the corner of her eye, and sighs as she realizes Billie Susan is okay. They're both still strapped in securely and the Jeep is sitting on its wheels. Her heart races in her chest, as she scans the road for the four-wheeler and Oliver and Virgil.

Billie Susan nods toward the back of the Jeep, and both women slowly turn around.

Virgil and Oliver are scrambling off the overturned four-wheeler. Both are empty handed.

Billie Susan reaches for the secure rifle behind the seat and hands it to Katie. "I got to see if I can limp this thing to the cabin. Don't hesitate to shoot to kill."

Katie doesn't say a word, as she takes the gun from the woman's trembling hands.

+++

The sound of gunfire stops Maddy in her tracks. She stares above her, as the birds screech, and make a mad dash from the south in her direction. Glancing around, she spots a small, homemade wooden deer blind ten feet off the road. Dragging the wagon behind her, she races toward it. She glances back at their tracks, and prays whoever is shooting doesn't see them or for a quick, heavy snow to cover them.

She steps inside and picks up the wagon, using it as a barrier against the door. She grabs up the axe and watches through the tiny slits in the wood.

Baby Girl whimpers as the cool breeze brushes against her uncovered cheeks.

"Sh … Baby. We have to be very quiet now," she whispers. She removes the makeshift gloves and feels the baby's cheeks.

They're warm.

She pulls the makeshift collar up around the baby's face once more and listens contentedly as the baby sucks lazily on her finger. She gazes back outside and listens intently for more gunshots. *You're so silly. There's probably some hunters out trying to scare up a mess of birds. That's why the birds were going nuts. Just relax. If nothing else we can make a fire in a couple of hours, warm up and then take off again.*

+++

"Have you heard anything?" My eyes never leave Olivia's face as Chanah nurses.

She sighs and shakes her head. "We will find her, I promise."

"It's okay. I know you guys are doing the best you can, but these guys are great at what they do. They're well connected. I'm guessing if you look hard enough in that alley way there are probably guns, drugs and more bodies hidden there. When this is all over I want to hire someone to come in and clean all that up."

Olivia, Kevin and Noah burst out laughing. Tears trace down their cheeks as they whimper and slap their sides.

+++

Deborah lifts her leg up and feels around the bottom of the hem. *Well, at least they let me keep my own clothes.* She grins as her hands slide around the small penknife still lodged in its hiding place. *Thank God they aren't real great at frisking. I know I'm not going to be killing anyone with this but maybe ...*

+++

Billie Susan's body pushes against the steering wheel with her whole strength, as the Jeep slips from side to side, almost toppling once more.

Thugga ... thugga ... thugga ... the tire slaps against the dirt road. Occasionally a spark flies as metal engages with metal or extra hard rocks.

Katie grips the gun and stares out the back window. "What do we do now?"

Billie Susan gazes in the back mirror as well as their surroundings. "I know where

there's a deer blind pretty close
to here. We got to make it there.
If we can make it there ... maybe
we won't have to do a standoff
from the Jeep."

Katie sighs. "The last time
I saw them, they were searching
for the guns. My guess is they
found them by now, and will be
heading our way."

"I reckon so. Well, nothing
to it but to do it. I hope you
can run 'cause this looks like
one of those times when we need
to outrun the zombies."

CHAPTER FORTY-TWO

The injured Jeep wheel slams
into a large crater and refuses
to budge.

Katie snags up one bag, as
well as the bow and quiver.

Grabbing up the full duffle
bag, Billie Susan slings it
across her back.

They race down the road.

"What exactly are we looking
for?" Katie asks, as she puffs
alongside her companion.

"A small wooden shelter, they use it for deer hunting. Pretty damn close to the road for deer hunting, but right now it's our best option until we're clear enough to make tracks for the cabin," Billie Susan answers.

Minutes later, the small shack looms ahead.

The roaring sound of the four-wheeler kills the quiet solitude of the air.

Neither say a word as they race toward the structure. Both gasp and grunt.

Tears slide down Katie's face, as the cold wind slaps against her cheeks.

Billie Susan reaches the door first and slams into it with her left shoulder. She gasps as she bounces off it, and lands face down in the snow and dirt. "What the hell?"

"Hello!" Katie calls out. "Please, let us in. We got two crazed hillbillies on our asses." Even as the words escape her lips, Katie realizes this too might be a great big mistake. She can't take it back now. It just has to be.

Maddy pulls the wagon away as well as the axe, and yanks the door open. She doesn't say a word as they slide in quickly. She replaces the barricade. Her hands shiver and shake, as she retreats to the corner with the baby.

"My name is Billie Susan and this is Katie. Are you Ole Mickey's latest?" Billie Susan puts out her hand.

"You know about Mickey?" Maddy gasps before taking the warm gloved hand.

Billie Susan nods before pulling her skull cap off and gloves and handing them to the cold, scared young woman. "I know and we're here to save you." She nods toward Katie.

Maddy slides the gloves on and pulls the cap over head. It's warm. It stops her shivering.

"How in the hell did you get this far?" Billie Susan asks, as she takes a seat on one of the old metal framed lawn chairs.

"I found a map. In fact I found a journal by Shoshana Meyers. Did you know she had been captive here too?" Katie asks, as she snuggles the baby closer, pulling the blanket back over her head.

"Oh my God, did you say Shoshana Meyers?" Katie gasps.

Maddy's eyes widen as she nods. "Yeah, do you read her books too?"

Katie sighs. "She was my sister-in-law."

Tears fill Maddy's eyes, she gazes between the huffing, puffing women and the baby. "Oh God, did she get killed? Did they kill her? Are they going to kill us?" Her heart skips a beat, as she backs up against the wooden wall.

Katie shakes her head. "No, sweetie, she's all right. It was my brother who died. No one killed Shoshana and no one is going to kill you. We just have to get back to the cabin.   Do you think you're up to it?"

"You mean running back? I don't know. It's almost five miles. I didn't know if we could even make it this far."

Katie faces Billie Susan. "Five miles?"

Billie Susan sighs and shakes her head. "I forgot how far it was, but if all serves me right ... I believe there is a tunnel under this blind. Let's see." Rising from her chair, she folds it and sweeps the dirt and snow away with the frozen metal.

All listen intently as the gunning engine nears.

"Oh God, please help us now," all three women voice softly. Katie and Maddy drop to their knees and dig at the hard soil until the metal hits a clang.

Billie Susan grins as she reaches down to the metal ring and pulls up.

Katie grabs the ring as well, and both pull with all their might.

The wood groans as it pops out of the dirt.

Grabbing a large flashlight from the bag, Katie illuminates the entrance.

Maddy wraps the baby back into the cradle board and slides down the frozen ladder, moving out of the way for the others.

Billie Susan drops the bags down into the hole.

Maddy grabs them up and drags them aside as Katie makes her way down.

"I know you're in there, you fucking bitch!" Oliver screams as the engine dies down.

Billie Susan grins as she fiddles with the lighter in her pocket. *You may get to us, you son of a bitches but it ain't gonna be here.* She pauses to light a rag, as she scans the small room. *Yeah, we got it all.* She lights it and tosses it toward the old wooden door. It smolders at first, smoking until a flicker of a tiny spark flashes back.

"I'm gonna come in there and get your scrawny fucking ass!" Virgil screams, as he pushes against the door.

The lawn chairs give little resistance as the wooden doorframe catches fire seconds before Billie Susan slams the tunnel door. Picking up the small two by four next to it, she slides it into place. She snatches up the second one as screams echo outside. *I'm guessing someone got a little too close to the fire. Dumbasses.* She slides the second one in place before making her way down to the others.

Katie hands her the other flashlight before they start the long trek.

"Oh God," Maddy gasps, as she stops dead in her tracks.

"What's wrong?" Billie Susan asks.

"What if they get to the cabin before us?" Katie answers.

"They'll get to the cabin before us all right, but they won't know where this thing comes out, you can be sure of that one. Ole Mickey kept that secret to the grave. I know one thing ... they ain't gonna find it."

Katie and Maddy nod as they push on.

+++

"We need to check into a hotel before we go out to the cabin," Olivia voices, as they pull off the highway into a Comfort Suites Hotel.

I want to fight this, but realize the last thing I need to do is face my biggest nightmare with cramped legs and needing to pee. *If Mickey is dead then the chances of Deborah being brought to the cabin are slim, right*? Tears fill my eyes, my sister, my baby sister. *How could I have put her in danger?*

"I think that's a great idea," Noah voices, as he pulls the baby carrier out of the car.

It takes me a few seconds to realize that I'm still sitting. Staring around me, I swipe the tears drying on my cheeks. They hurt, the tears not the cheeks, but as soon as the bitter cold reaches them, they ache too.

"I'll go get the rooms." Kevin heads inside as Olivia makes her way toward me.

"I'm guessing there hasn't been any new texts." I sigh and take her arm.

She shakes her head. "I'm sorry. Let's get you inside and get you something to eat. It's going to be dark pretty soon. We need to get out there before then.

I nod and take her hand. *Yes, we have to get in there before nighttime. That's when all the crazies really come out.*

+++++

Deborah leans back into the faux leather cushion and sighs.

"Are you sure you don't want something to eat?" Mr. Zander asks, as he waves a large meat filled sandwich under her nose.

She bites her bottom lip until it bleeds, as the bile in her stomach rises up the back of her throat. She coughs and shakes her head, as she tries to focus on the wall behind him. They're in a small camper of some sort.

It's roomy like a small trailer house, but obviously still a tin can on wheels.

"You fucking Jews, won't eat this ... won't eat that." Deborah shudders and gags. "It's not that," she whispers. Her body aches as she tries to keep herself in an upright position. She's thankful she has a table top to lean upon.

"Oh, yeah, they dosed you pretty good, didn't they? Those guys think they got to give an elephant dose to everyone. I keep trying to tell them they don't, but they won't listen. They keep acting like the dope is stepped on, but not our stuff. It is pure all the way." He chuckles before taking a huge bite.

"Huh?" Deborah's eyebrows furrow together as everything goes fuzzy. *Please, eyes, please focus. Now what is he saying about drugs?* Her head throbs behind her eyeballs and for a second she's sure her eardrums will burst with the low hum of the tires against the asphalt. She sighs.

"It's our own little mixture. It's guaranteed to get someone off," Mr. Zander remarks before taking another bite.

"Why me?" Deborah asks.

"Because we can't draw out your sister without you," Mr. Zander answers.

"Why do you need my sister?" Deborah asks, her ankle chain clatters against the floor as she kicks anxiously. Her toes slam into the wooden baseboard. She frowns and suppresses the urge to scream. *I'm going to kill this bastard if I ever get the chance. I'm going to wipe that smug little smirk right off his frigging face. He'll think fucking Jews when I'm through with him.* Deborah doesn't say a word as she smiles and nods.

CHAPTER FORTY-THREE

Staring out the window, I try to remember everything about the cabin I can.

"Are you all right?" Noah asks.

"I'm okay. I'm just preparing myself for war." I chuckle and wink at him.

+++

Maddy drops to her knees and gasps.

"Are you all right?" Billie Susan grabs Maddy's left arm and tried to help her up.

"It's really weird. I just had a cold shiver run up and down my spine like someone was walking over my grave."

Katie gasps. "Sweetie, let's not talk about graves yet. We're underground, and we aren't safe yet until we get back to town."

"Okay, I'm okay. I think I need to eat something."

Billie Susan pulls an energy bar from her pouch and hands it to Maddy.

Maddy inhales it in three bites.

"Girlfriend, when we get out of here I promise to take you to the best restaurant in town, New York City town," Katie states, as she helps the young woman back up.

Maddy checks on the sleeping baby before they make their way toward the house.

"This thing is huge, where did this thing come from?" Katie asks. She flashes the flashlight down the tunnel. It's at least six feet tall, and at least four feet wide. The dirt is packed so tight, it's almost like rock. Every eight feet is marked with two-by-four crossbeams.

"I don't know the whole history behind it, but it goes back to either the Civil War or the Revolutionary War. It's been used to help soldiers and slaves escape, as well as angry hillbillies." Billie Susan shakes her head, as they race across the dirt floor. The flashlights illuminate the way. No one says a word as several large snakes slither past.

Spiders hang from the wooden rafters as well as other hibernating animals.

+++

"Can't you get that damn thing started?" Oliver asks, as they stand around the four-wheeler.

"The damn wheel is flat and it looks like the fucking rock," Virgil points toward a large boulder, "punched a hole in the gas tank. Did you find the guns?"

Oliver grins as he points to the weapons leaning against the large brush.

"Grab 'em up and let's head that way. Those bitches couldn't

have gotten too far. I'm hornier
than a three horned bull."

+++

"Are we even close?" Mr. Big
asks, as he stares out the
window.

Mr. Zander sighs. "We just
pulled off the highway. We should
be at the house in about an
hour."

"Bring me the bitch." Mr.
Big licks his lips and grins. He
tugs at the tightness in his
pants. *Might as well have a
little fun before we get there.*

Mr. Zander steps out the
door. He leaves it open as he
makes his way toward Deborah.
"It's time," he sings.

Deborah shakes her head and
pulls back. "No," she whispers.

Mr. Zander leans down, and
snaps open the lock on the table
post. "You gonna keep him
occupied. If he says suck my dick
you better fucking ask him how
deep. If he says he's going to

fuck you in the ass, you better roll over."

Tears roll down Deborah's cheeks. "Never."

Grabbing her arm, Mr. Zander snatches a syringe from the sink and plunges it into her vein.

She whimpers and reaches under the table. Snatching the penknife from her hiding place, she slams it into Mr. Zander's right ear.

He screams and drops the empty syringe on the ground. He falls to his knees jabbing the needle into his kneecap. Blood spurts from his ear as he cups it with his right hand while trying to pulls the knife out with the left.

Deborah leaps to her feet and pushes the screaming man with all her might.

His crumpled body falls over the sink, as he drops to the floor. He grips the bloody penknife in his hand. He coughs and gags as vomit spews across Deborah's blouse and his pants.

"You sorry piece of shit," she whispers, as she stomps her foot down on his penis and grabs for the penknife.

He blindly stabs at her as she falls back against the table, and slams her head into the couch cushion.

"No!" Deborah screams as everything goes black.

+++

Deborah's hands reach up to push the heavy weight off her chest. *Oh God one of the kids brought home a full grown Saint Bernard and now it's trying to sleep with me. What the hell?* "Get off me, you crazy dog." She pushes with all her might and giggles as he refuses to move.

Heavy breathing and slobbering over her breasts make her eyes pop open, as well as her lips as a scream escapes them. "What the fuck are you doing?" Even before she lets the words slip from her mouth, she cringes as his hardness shoves deeper inside her.

"I'm fucking you, you stupid fucking cunt. That's probably why you're so good and tight. God, I can't wait to flip your ass over and get a shot at that. I'm gonna shoot my load so deep into you, you'll be shooting it out your mouth and nose." He moans into her ear.

She grips the slippery cloth as she glances around the room. *Thank God there's light in here.* She spots Mr. Zander's crumpled body on the floor. Blood flowers out around his torso, and he doesn't move.

"Oh God." Circling his thick fingers around her neck, he tightens them with a grin. "You're an even better fuck than your sister."

Deborah's eyes widen as she lets her breathing drop down to shallow gasps. *Oh no you don't, you aren't going to kill me today. You may rape me, but you definitely won't be killing me*

today, you low life piece of
scum. "Fuck you."

   Mr. Big snickers and tosses
his head back revealing pearly
whites with a few flashes of gold
in the back. "Yeah, baby, I'm
fucking you. When I'm done with
you, I'm gonna do what that
bastard Mickey was supposed to do
to your sister. They'll never
find your body." Loosening his
hands from around her neck, he
buries his head between her
breasts, biting her flesh until
blood pours.

   Wincing, tears streak down
her cheeks as she spots the small
snub nosed .38 on the head board.
If I can just distract him for
like two seconds, and pray to God
that it's loaded … maybe, just
maybe … Tears drench her face as
she thinks about never seeing her
husband or children again.
Shoshana and Chanah, where are
they? *Please help me, God, make*
me the best actress ever ….
Please.

   She gasps and moans. "Oh
baby, fuck me harder. Oh God,
your cock is going to split me in

two. It's so big. Please baby, whatever you do, don't fuck me in my virgin ass. It would probably make me cum so hard …. Make me scream."

"Now that's what I like to hear. Now you are getting it." He grins and pulls out, flipping her over on her stomach. Slapping her backside, he makes his way toward her.

Closing her eyes, she reaches for the gun. She listens for his yelp of happiness as he finds his target.

"No," she whispers so softly, she knows he won't hear. She cocks it and lets her hand slide down beside her. Intense pain fills her pelvis as he shoves himself inside her. For a second she isn't sure she made a mistake as the pain engulfs her pelvis making her heart skip a beat. She wants to scream, feels it deep in her throat, but refuses to let go.

Feeling resistance, she pulls the trigger.

He screams, leaps back and grabs his inner thigh as blood spurts across her back and sheets, dripping down his leg.

She whirls around, gasping and crying. "You sorry son-of-a-bitch, I'm the last woman you're ever going to rape."

+++

Maddy, Katie and Billie Susan reach the first ladder.

"Are you sure they aren't going to be waiting for us?" Katie asks.

"No, I'm not sure. That's why I think Maddy should stay here with the baby until we make sure it's clear." Billie Susan stacks some supplies right beside the ladder.

"How do we know we'll be able to come back for her?" Katie stares into the other woman's eyes.

"I'm scared." Maddy backs up against the wall. She cuddles the baby against her. Her arms tremble as she drops to the ground. "Please don't make me go up there. I'll just stay here. I'm safer here. The baby is safer here, please."

"I promise, we will be back to get her." She leans over and kisses Katie's soft pink lips.

Katie sighs and turns around, handing the young woman the small caliber gun and a box of bullets. "We'll be back, soonest."

Billie Susan grabs her arm before Maddy can answer. Billie Susan and Katie grab up their weapons and start up the ladder.

+++

Virgil and Oliver race into the cabin. Kicking in doors, and knocking over furniture, they make their way toward the upstairs.

"Where the fuck are those bitches?" Virgil hisses.

"We'll find 'em. They couldn't go past us. They have to

be here." Oliver steps toward the bedroom door and grins. "This is where he keeps 'em."

"Well, don't just sit there, open 'er up. Open up, bitches, 'cause we is gonna be fucking tonight." Virgil slams into the door knocking it off its hinges and shattering the wood.

"Where the hell is them bitches?" Oliver asks as they stare around the empty room.

CHAPTER FORTY-FOUR

Picking up the wooden bat, Deborah aims it toward the big man's head. Heavy sobs wrack her body, as she grabs for her pants up off the floor. Already she knows she's bleeding, and the intense anal pain makes her want to drop to her to the floor and lie in a fetal position, but she fights it.

Mr. Big grabs for her, and she slams the bat into his fingers.

Where the hell did the gun go? When I shot him it was kicked out of my hand by his knee jerk, but now I really frigging need it. She glances around and doesn't spot it before Mr. Big lunges for her once more. Blood spurts from the wound in his thigh, but he makes no move to stop it.

"No, I don't think so." She races toward the door, stumbling over the wadded up rug and Mr. Zander's body. Pushing the door open, she slams it shut and looks for something to block it.

She tosses the pillows and cushions in the doorway seconds before glancing back down at the bat lying next to the other door. The door to freedom. She didn't want to leave jammed against his door. You never know when you're going to need a great hitting bat. She glances around once more and spots a shotgun as well as another bat. Wedging the second bat against the door, she picks up the gun.

Just a twelve gauge but hopefully enough to stop whatever might try to get at her. Deborah's body aches as she makes her way to the door. She races to the front of the camper to see if she can distract the driver. A wall stands between them. "Damn." She listens for pounding on the bedroom door but there isn't any.

She dashes toward the door leading outside, feeling the vehicle slow down. She inhales deeply and loads a cartridge into the chamber. She shoves the extra box of shells into a small pouch she picked up from beside the sink. Grabbing everything up, Deborah pushes through the door before they come to a complete stop.

Leaping out the door, Deborah races toward a clump of bushes and trees. She shivers as her bare feet sail through the soft layer of snow. It doesn't stop her. She'd rather freeze than be with those evil men ever again.

"What the hell?" the young emo man jumps from the truck, and dashes toward Deborah. He zips up the heavy jacket, as he closes in on her.

"Unless you want to die, you need to turn around and take off back to your boss," Deborah states, as she twirls around and aims the gun at his chest.

"You aren't going to kill me," the young man grins. His emo hair flips back into his eyes, blocking his sight as he aims the 9 mm at her head.

"I guess we both die then 'cause I ain't going to put it down until you blow off my head," Deborah doesn't blink. Grasping the butt of the gun deep into her left shoulder, she's happy that Moshe demanded she learn to use a gun. She inhales deeply as she lets her trigger finger slide up and down the trigger.

"Drop the weapon," a male voice screams from the camper.

"No!" Deborah yells back.

"It's okay, we want to help you," a familiar female voice calls out.

Tears flow down Deborah's cheeks as she recognizes the voice, it's Olivia.

Emo man shoves the gun into Deborah's chest, pushing her down to the ground.

She flips over a fallen, rotten log and the shotgun flies from her hands, lying ten feet from her reach."Damn."

In a flash, he's in her face. The gun is less than an inch from her nose.

She doesn't blink, as she stares into his eyes.

"Let her go, asshole," three voices scream.

"Not until I know I'm safe," Emo man yells back.

"You let her up, and we let you come with us to jail. You tell us enough, and we might be able to cut you a deal. "

Emo man shakes his head. Tears stream down his cheeks, he frowns and turns the gun toward his left temple, pulling the trigger.

Deborah screams as blood and brains shower her covering her face and hair.

His lean, bloody body lands squarely on hers. Her hands tremble as she shoves at him with all her might, and finds it impossible to move his dead weight.

"We got you!" someone hollers in the distance.

She tries to call back, but suddenly the world goes black.

+++

Billie Susan eases the trapdoor open and peers out. She sighs as she realizes they're in the garage. "It's okay, we're outside." She opens the door all the way, and helps Katie up through the rabbit hole. "I hope you ain't got a problem with shooting to kill."

"How are we going to get out of here?" Katie's heart skips a beat.

"There's a satellite phone in the attic. It runs off solar power. We get up there. We got it made. We get rid of those assholes, and we can make it."

Katie nods and lets her heart sink into her stomach. *I guess it really can get worse, can't it? Brother, what the hell did you get me into now?*

+++

Deborah opens her eyes and gasps. "Shoshana," she whispers.

I race toward her, my eyes ever mindful of the pitfalls that show up in most horror movies about now. So far, so good.

Olivia dashes across the snow, leaping over the fallen branches and lumps along the path until she reaches her.

I gaze back at Noah and wave before making my way toward my sister. "I'm on my way."

My heart races in my chest as I follow Olivia's path. The gunshot echoes in the quietude even before I feel the sharpness slash into my left shoulder blade. I gasp and for ten seconds I'm flying like an angel. My face slams into the snow and everything goes dark.

+++

Katie and Billie Susan recheck their weapons before tiptoeing out of the shed. They crisscross through the ten yards to the front door. Neither says a word as they make their way in.

"I still don't see any fucking bitches," Oliver whines loudly from the second floor.

Billie Susan points toward the curtained-off space under the sink. It's just large enough for her.

Katie nods and dives into it. She takes shallow breaths, as she listens for the loud thumps of heavy boots on the staircase. *Where did Billie Susan go? How the hell are we going to get past* them? *Oh God, please let this all be okay.*

Her heart skips a beat as she spots the arrow hanging off of Virgil's boot. She aims the gun as best she can without thrusting it through the curtain. *Nothing to see here, just keep moving along. Hey guys, maybe we're still on the road. Why don't you nut jobs go check that out again?* Even as the words race through her brain, she knows this isn't going to happen. It never does. Hillbillies never give up.

"I know they're in here," Oliver states. "Where else could they have gone?"

Virgil drops down into the large, overstuffed sofa and pulls the arrow out of his boot. Grasping with all his might, he yanks the boot from his swelling foot.

"What the hell? Did she actually get you?"

Virgil sneers at his cousin as he rips the torn blackened sock from his foot. Dried blood cakes the top of his foot and sock. "Stupid fucking bitch. I get my hand on them, I don't even think I want to fuck 'em. I just want to blow their heads off."

Oliver snickers and slaps the back of his thighs. "How many times you gonna get shot by a woman?"

It's all Katie can do to keep from leaping out and yelling "just one more time" as she gives each of them a blast from her double barreled shotgun.

CHAPTER FORTY-FIVE

"You can't die! You can't die!" a familiar voice screams into my ear. I blink twice before I close them again. My back and chest ache. It almost feels like an elephant stomped on my body, almost. It's all I can do to take the next strong breath. I try to open my eyes but they hurt.

A baby whimpering in the background drags me out of the fog that feels like sleep.

"Chanah!"

"Come on, Shoshana, you're okay," Deborah whispers in my left ear.

I inhale deeply and cringe as the pain sears through my chest again. "It hurts," I gasp.

"Shoshana, I'm okay."

I grin. *My baby sister is okay. My baby is okay. I'm alive.*

"I think she's hungry," Noah voices.

Oh God, the baby is hungry. Opening my eyes as wide as possible, I sit up and gaze around the room. "Where am I?" I spot Chanah in Noah's arms.

She's chewing on her fist and whining.

"Was I shot?" I ask, feeling my chest and body. The stiffness of the body armor under my coat nearly knocks me out again.

"You were. Aren't you glad we talked you into wearing a bullet proof vest?" Kevin asks.

Olivia steps over and wraps her arms around me. "You really scared the hell out of us," she whispers into my ear. "Let's get that heavy thing off you so you can feed that precious baby of yours."

It takes me a minute to piece everything together as I stare at Deborah taking the baby from Noah.

"Are you okay?" Deborah steps toward me. "You don't look too good."

"I feel a little confused." Tears stream down my cheeks and I giggle despite my heart sitting in the back of my throat.

"Well, you are in the back of the DEA van. Apparently they and a few other task force reps have been watching this place."

"How did I get shot?"

+++

"Well, I think we best get out of here and hit the road!" Virgil shouts as he points toward a slight movement under the sink.

Oliver nods. "Yeah, I bet them bitches are frozen out there. Nothing like frozen bitches to make my day."

Katie closes her eyes and holds her breath, praying they will leave soonest. She listens for their distinctive stomping and the slamming of the door. She counts to twenty before easing herself out of her hiding place. Glancing around, she lets out a heavy sigh as she drops the gun to her side, still cocked.

"Gotcha!" Oliver screams, as he leaps out from the other room. Virgil is on his heels. His hands are up in the air as he storms toward her.

Katie jams the gun into her shoulder and pulls the trigger. Popping another round into the chamber, she aims toward Virgil and lets loose.

Screams echo against the wooden walls as both barrels hit hardened chests, shoving the two giants back against each other. They fall to the floor, knocking over several chairs and a floor lamp. Blood splatters across the rug hitting within inches of Katie's foot.

Tears stream down her cheeks as she unloads the spent cartridges and reloads. Aiming for their heads, she stands there. Her hands tremble beneath the metal and wood, but she doesn't take her eyes off them. "I dare you to move now, you scumbags!"

Virgil moans and reaches for her. His dark eyes are wide with fear and pain. He coughs and gasps for air. He jabs his hand against the floor to push himself up, but his face turns ghostly white before he falls back. He inhales deeply, screams and stops moving. His eyes roll up into the back of his head and blood dribbles from his open lips.

Katie gasps and makes her way toward the men. *Okay, this is the part in the movie where I'm usually screaming at the idiot on the screen to get the hell out of there but I can't. I have to find Billie Susan. Where the hell is Billie Susan?* She gazes around the room once more, and realizes if she is going to get out of the room then she must go past the two men.

Shaking her head, she aims the gun at Virgil and makes her way toward the stairs. "Billie Susan! Where are you?" She steps around Virgil, thankful he won't be moving. She stares at Oliver and grins. *You ain't getting these dumb bitches, are you?* She steps her right foot over his large body nearly doing the splits.

Oliver slips a hunting knife out of his sleeve and slams it into her left foot. "Gotcha!"

Her screams echo off the cabin walls, as pain fills her foot and brain. Kill races through her mind and it's all she can do to keep from slamming the butt of the gun into the man's face. But that wouldn't kill him. It wouldn't stop him, only piss him off. No, he needs to be stopped.

He grins up at her as he reaches toward her crotch with his other hand

Katie twists around and shoves the business end of the gun into Oliver's mouth.

He grins around the cold metal before snagging the top of her free leg.

"I said no," she whispers, as she pulls the trigger. She smirks as his brain and blood splatters up her leg and across the floor. Blood flowers into the dirt covered floor. Her knees buckle and she slumps to the floor, landing hard on her victim. Her own blood mixes with his, as the pain in her foot sears itself into her brain.

Billie Susan races down the stairs, her own gun at the ready. She smiles when she sees the two dead bodies. "Good girl."

Wincing, Katie sets the weapon down beside her. Tears fill her eyes, as she reaches for the knife imprisoning her foot to the floor. "I … can't … get … up," she whispers. Grasping the knife with both hands, she winces as they slide right off. They drop to her side as bile rises to the back of her throat and threaten to spill across Oliver's blood soaked face and chest. "It hurts."

Billie Susan shoves something black into her pocket before grasping the knife with both hands and ripping it from the floor, still embedded in Katie's foot.

"Don't forget Maddy and the baby," Katie gasps before everything goes dark.

+++

Maddy finishes off the third energy bar just as the baby pulls off her left breast. Maddy covers herself up, and slides the sleeping child back into the cradle board and straps her in. *How long have they been gone? Oh*

God, what if they don't come back for me? What should I do? I can't stay down here any longer. It's cold, freezing cold. I guess the sun has gone down now. She pulls the holey jacket from her shoulders and wraps it around the baby. "I guess I better head back the way I came."

She shoves the energy bar wrapper into her pocket. For something that is supposed to give her energy, she doesn't feel any better. She's cold and tired. It's all she can do to keep from lying down on the dirt floor and going to sleep, eternal sleep. "I can't sleep now. I have to find us a way out of here. We have to go to the road."

Standing up, she grabs the backpack and slings it over her shoulder. She glances back up at the trapdoor before trudging away.

Suddenly the trapdoor opens, Maddy's heart takes a leap as her feet prepare to race down the tunnel.

"Don't run!" Billie Susan yells down. "It's okay. We're going to come down and help you get up here."

Maddy slowly moves back into the light and stares up into its brightness. Covering her eyes with her hands, she grins as she spots Billie Susan's now familiar face. "Can you hurry it up? I'm about to freeze my backbone off down here."

Billie Susan giggles as she grabs onto the ladder and slides down. She wraps her arms around the young woman, as she attaches a lifeline to her and the baby. Pulling the strap between the young woman's legs, she checks the safety harness.

"Are they dead?"

Billie Susan nods. "The police are here. They're going to want to hear your story. Girlfriend, you're going home."

Tears fill her eyes and roll down her cheeks, Maddy shakes her head. "I ain't got no home."

"Oh, baby girl, you got a home. I guarantee … you got a home."

CHAPTER FORTY-SIX

Gazing around the hotel suite, I grin. Deborah and Noah are cooing at the babies in their arms. Deborah holds Chanah while Noah holds Baby Girl. It's remarkable how much the two girls look alike. Chanah is a little smaller but just as beautiful as Baby Girl

Maddy steps out of the bathroom wrapped in a thick, plush bathrobe and new pajamas.

"Are you sure you don't want to go to the hospital?" Billie Susan asks, as she follows the young woman toward the recliner next to the couch. "In fact, I don't understand why all of you aren't in the hospital."

"Please, what can they do? I'm fine now that I'm warm and my baby is safe." Maddy grins at me and winks.

Katie points toward her heavily bandaged foot and grins. "No way, they spent enough time sewing it up and all. I think that tetanus shot said it all," she whimpers as she tries to lift her left arm and fails.

Everyone sniggers.

"Oh, wait, I have something for you." Maddy leaps to her feet. "Where's my backpack? I've got something in my backpack for you, Ms. Shoshana."

"You mean that ratty old thing?" Deborah points toward a lump under the coffee table.

Olivia picks it up, and hands it to the young woman.

"Thank you. I have it in here somewhere. I checked it twice while we were being checked out in the hospital. One of the cops tried to take it away from me, but I told them it was mine." She eyes me as her clean hands slip into the cold, dirty pack and pulls out a dirt covered journal. Rising to her feet, she makes her way toward me. Her eyes are wide and teeth white with her big grin, as she hands it to me. "If it weren't for you leaving this and them not finding it, I would have never had the courage to leave. Your map could have taken me all the way to town if I'd had to follow it. You're my favorite writer. You always gave me courage, even when I was trapped."

My heart skips a beat before thumping loudly in my chest, almost too loud for me to hear what the others are saying. My chest and back still aches from the impact of the bullet into the bullet proof vest. Who knew getting shot with one of those on would still cause so much pain, but at least it didn't go through. The pride in my face can't take away the happiness I have for knowing we had to go to the cabin. We had to save her.

"That's my sister … the horror writer. At least in this story we all come out alive and well," Deborah states.

"I still don't understand everything. Like why did they take me?"

"Well," Olivia sighs, as she slides down into the desk chair beside me. She eyes the others around the room: Deborah, Noah, Kevin, Katie, Billie Susan, the two babies and me. "It seems it had something to do with your last book, the one that became a best seller especially after you disappeared."

I cock my eyebrows and stare into her eyes. "Huh? Blood River? What about it?"

Kevin nods. "That's the one."

"Right before Mr. Big died he confessed that he felt like you wrote it about him. You know, a drug and human trafficking story based in New York City wrapped around the mob and key politicians?"

I sigh. "Yeah, I don't remember every line I've ever written, but I definitely recall the plots." I smiggle and shake my head. "So, I still don't get how Stan was involved or my agent."

"Well, that's the tricky part. He didn't tell us all the details. I guess your sister is a better shot than she thought. When we tried to move him the bullet in his leg lodged into an artery, and he bleed out seconds after his main confession."

"And what was that?" Deborah asks, winking at me.

"To never mess with a couple of mean Jewish girls," Noah snickers.

Everyone breaks out laughing and slapping their legs.

"He probably should have said that, but actually what he said was he wished he had killed you two when he had the chance. He refused to say what Stan had to do with it all, but the bastard kept records so maybe it is in his own writings."

"A couple of hours ago, the NYPD as well as several DEA task forces busted into about ten holding pens. Several were here in West Virginia and at least three were in Miami. They freed almost two hundred young people, as well as taking in almost a billion dollars in drugs. Guess where most of them were?"

I shake my head as I let the information sink in. *The end of my nightmare saved so many others, thank God. My captivity wasn't in vain. It was for a reason. It's always for a reason. I guess truth is stranger than fiction after all.*

"It was in the buildings surrounding your alley, Blood River Alley, or so they've come to call it now. It seems that you were right there in the hub. It's almost as if you knew they were there, and was just trying to figure out how to save them," Billie Susan states.

"You know what the strangest part is?"

"I know," Maddy chimes in. "You actually did research in that alley, didn't you? How many times did you go to that alley before you wrote that book?"

"Probably as many times as I went there to sleep or hide when I was homeless. Every time I sat in that alley I felt like I was being transported to another time and place." I sigh.

Tears slide down her cheeks, Maddy nods. "You were hearing all the victims screaming at you from the rafters to save them from blood alley."

Special Acknowledgement:

I want to acknowledge all those lost souls who have disappeared due to being kidnapped either for sale in the sex trade or just to be made a slave. Maybe someday this will no longer exist. Too many have been lost to the depravity of other human beings.

Thank you for reading.

Barbara (Meyers)
Pappan/babylonia,
Facebook/Twitter/Fanstory

(lilcoyote2002@peoplepc.com)